Praise for the award myst

MW00951594

"Joe Cosentino has a unique and fabulous gift. His writing is flawless, and his use of farce, along with his convoluted plot-lines, will have you guessing until the very last page, which makes his books a joy to read. His books are worth their weight in gold, and if you haven't discovered them yet you are in for a rare treat." *— Divine Magazine*

"a combination of Laurel and Hardy mixed with Hitchcock and *Murder She Wrote*...Loaded with puns and one-liners...Right to the end, you are kept guessing, and the conclusion still has a surprise in store for you." *— Optimumm Book Reviews*

"adventure, mystery, and romance with every page.... Funny, clever, and sweet....I can't find anything not to love about this series....This read had me laughing and falling in love....Nicky and Noah are my favorite gay couple." *— Urban Book Reviews*

"For fans of Joe Cosentino's hilarious mysteries, this is another vintage story with more cheeky asides and sub plots right left and centre....The story is fast paced, funny and sassy. The writing is very witty with lots of tongue-in-cheek humour....Highly recommended." *— Boy Meets Boy Reviews*

"This delightfully sudsy, colorful cast of characters would rival that of any daytime soap opera, and the character exchanges are rife with sass, wit and cagey sarcasm....As the pages turn quickly, the author keeps us hanging until the startling end." *— Edge Media Network*

"A laugh and a murder, done in the style we have all come to love....This had me from the first paragraph....Another wonderful story with characters you know and love!"
— *Crystals Many Reviewers*

"These two are so entertaining....Their tactics in finding clues and the crazy funny interactions between characters keeps the pages turning. For most of the book if I wasn't laughing I was grinning." — *Jo and Isa Love Books*

"Superb fun from start to finish, for me this series gets stronger with every book and that's saying something because the benchmark was set so very high with book 1."
— *Three Books Over the Rainbow*

"The Nicky and Noah Mysteries series are perfect for fans of the Cozy Mystery sub-genre. They mix tongue-in-cheek humor, over-the-top characters, a wee bit of political commentary, and suspense into a sweet little mystery solved by Nicky and Noah, theatre professors for whom all the world's a stage." — *Prism Book Alliance*

DON'T MISS ANY OF THE NICKY AND NOAH
MYSTERIES BY JOE COSENTINO!

Drama Queen
Drama Muscle
Drama Cruise
Drama Luau
Drama Detective
Drama Fraternity
Drama Castle
Drama Dance (coming soon)
Drama Faerie (coming soon)
Drama Runway (coming soon)
Drama Christmas (coming soon)

Drama
Castle

A NICKY AND NOAH MYSTERY

Joe Cosentino

Copyright © 2019 Joe Cosentino

ISBN-13: 9781792043819

Printed in the United State of America
First Edition, 2019

This is a work of fiction. All characters, places and events are from the author's very vivid imagination and should not be confused with fact. Any resemblance to persons, living or dead, events or places is purely coincidental.

All rights reserved. No part of this publication may be reproduced in any material form, whether by printing, photocopying, scanning or otherwise without the written permission of the author.

The content of this book is not meant to diagnose, treat, or prevent any illness or condition. This novel is for mature readers.

Cover art by Jesús Da Silva
Nicky & Noah Logo by Holly McCabe
Cover and interior design by Fred Wolinsky

★

To Fred for everything,
to the readers who begged
for another Nicky and Noah mystery,
and to everyone who loves a good castle,
or at least a good queen.

Cast of Characters

Cast and Crew of
When the Wind Blows Up Your Kilt
It's Time for a Scotch

Nicky Abbondanza
Professor of Play Directing
Director

Noah Oliver
Nicky's husband
Professor of Acting
Acting Coach, *Oliver*

Martin Anderson
Theatre Department Head
Prof. of Theatre Management
Screenwriter

Ruben Markinson
Martin's husband
Producer

Taavi Kapule
Nicky and Noah's son
younger Roddy Conall

Barclay Conall
current owner and
manager of Conall Castle
Ainsley Conall

Magnus Conall
Barclay's middle brother
accountant at Conall Castle
Archibald Conall

Fergus Conall
Barclay's youngest brother
restaurant manager at
Conall Castle
Angus Conall

Moira Conall
Barclay's wife
desk clerk at Conall Castle
Fiona Conall

Hamish MacAlastair
waiter at Conall Castle
Fergus's fiancé
Prince Jock

Brody Naughton
head of Housekeeping at
Conall Castle
Prince Bruce

Lairie Naughton
Brody's daughter
Aggie

Donal Blair
waiter at Conall Castle
older Roddy Conall

THE FAMILY

Bonnie (Mom) and Scott (Dad) Oliver
Noah's parents

Valentina (Mama) and Giacomo (Papa) Abbondanza
Nicky's Parents

Tony Abbondanza
Nicky's brother

EX-CARETAKER OF THE CONALL ABBEY

Ewan Baird

POLICE SERVICE OF SCOTLAND

Chief Inspector Lennox Frazier

Inspector Owen Steward

WE'LL NEVER TELL

Two brownies (elves)
Three Brahan Seers (psychics)

Sidhe (fairy)
Shellycoat (bogeyman)

CHAPTER ONE

Ainsley Conall, the thirty-five-year-old lord of the manor, stood on the grassy moor surveying his property. He watched the mist spread to the nearby golden cliff, emerald mountains, and white-capped turquoise sea. His tunic, kilt, hose, and shoulder cloak matched the tall, strapping man's long auburn hair and striking emerald eyes. The leather sporran hanging from a chain over the impressive lump at his groin proudly bore the Conall family crest — three lions. As he rested his size-ten leather brogue on a rock, Ainsley proudly gazed out at the ancient lighthouse, old abbey, and most importantly Conall Castle standing majestically in the distance. This was his heritage, his pride, and his joy.

An eastern wind blew the kilt up his back, exposing his melon-like bubble butt.

"Cut! We'll save that for the blooper reel."

I always wanted to say that. But I didn't think I'd be uttering those words on a mountaintop at the northernmost tip of Scotland. I'm Nicky Abbondanza, Associate Professor of Play Directing at Treemeadow College, a private college plagued by murder in scenic Vermont. How did I get to Scotland, the land of men in kilts? After directing a play at Treemeadow College that moved to Broadway, I helmed a slasher film, which to nobody's surprise was ignored by the Academy Award voters. However, Barclay Conell, the owner of Conell Castle and Hotel in Scotland, caught it while scrolling through one-star instant-play movies on his computer. It wasn't so much that Barclay was impressed with my artistry. The film's low budget and one-week production schedule caught the green in his eyes. You see Barclay was also the author of *The Lord of the Castle*, a five-hundred-and-thirty-eight-page novel that could turn an insomniac into Rip Van Winkle. Propelled by his novel's high local sales, Barclay decided a film adaptation was in order—even when a local fisherman confessed he had bought up all the novels as gifts for unsuspecting fishermen in hopes of sinking the competition's ships. When Barclay's emails to Z-list celebrities went unanswered, undaunted in his cinematic pursuit, Barclay decided to star in the film version himself—playing his 1745 ancestor, Ainsley Conall. His wife, Moira (an unemployed actress currently working as his desk clerk), finally got an acting gig as Ainsley's devoted wife. For reality sake, and to keep peace in the family, Barclay's middle brother, Magnus (the hotel's accountant), was cast as Ainsley's middle brother and pal, Archibald. Finally, Barclay's youngest brother, Fergus (the hotel's restaurant manager), didn't have much of a stretch to play Ainsley's youngest brother and little buddy, Angus. And to keep the budget anemic, Lairie Naughton, the fourteen-year-old daughter of the hotel's head of Housekeeping, was slated for the role of the devoted young maid, Aggie.

Barclay took no reservations at the hotel for a week in June and made me an offer I couldn't refuse: a four-figure salary, a film budget as thin as a vegan with a malfunctioning juicer, and a one-week shooting schedule. How could I say no? So, I continued the casting by adding my ten-year-old adopted son from Hawaii, Taavi, as Ainsley's adored son, Roddy. Before a divorce was threatened, I hired my husband of four years, Assistant Professor of Acting at Treemeadow College, Noah Oliver, to play Roddy's noble tutor, Oliver, and to serve as the film's acting coach. I decided to cast the smaller roles once we got to the castle.

There was the small, or not so small, matter of the film adaptation. Barclay's attempt was as ponderous and heavy (pun intended) as his novel. So, my best friend and department head, Professor of Theatre Management Martin Anderson, wrote the screenplay, or as Ruben Markinson, Martin's husband and our producer, said, "the foul-play." With the excitement of a conservative politician nixing environmental laws, Martin went to work loading the script with scandal, seduction, and assassination. *Try saying that three times fast.* His new title: *When the Wind Blows Up Your Kilt, You Need a Scotch.*

Craving a family vacation, I asked my parents and Noah's parents to come along. My folks had just developed gluten-free, wheat-free, sugar-free, butter-free, chocolate-free, and preservative-free pastries at their bakery that cost next to nothing to make but were incredibly popular. With their sudden windfall, like the Wizard of Oz, they didn't want to leave Kansas. However, Noah's parents in Wisconsin jumped in faster than a televangelist buying a second mansion after pledge week.

So, Noah, Taavi, Martin, Ruben, and I took a plane from Vermont to New York, where we met up with Mom and Dad who flew in from Wisconsin. At the airport, Mom took pictures of us and texted them to her best friend Judy in Wisconsin, while Dad told us all about the movie he saw on the flight — *Airport*. Then we all flew from New York to Edinburgh. Next, we boarded a train from Edinburgh to Dunnett Head. A ferry took us from Dunnett Head to Conall, and a van drove us to Conall Castle. Needless to say, I was worn out upon arrival. However, as a one-man man, I had to keep up with my younger (only by seven years) gorgeous husband who, by the way, has long hair like golden heather and aqua eyes like the sea.

Okay, for you gentle readers new to my series, I'll tell you a little secret. Actually, it's not so little. I'm thirty-nine, tall, muscular, with dark hair, long sideburns, emerald eyes, a Roman nose, and a nearly foot-long penis. Thankfully Noah has become quite…open to new things.

Having exposed that (not literally), let's get back to my story. On the first day of shooting, despite being in Scotland, Noah and I stood next to the camera operator, wearing our customary dress shirts, slacks, and blazers. We were on a gorgeous kelly-green meadow staring at Barclay's equally gorgeous beach ball bum. *Try saying that three times fast.*

Martin, somewhere between seventy and extinction, was behind us in a cranberry bowtie and sweater vest, glued to his screenplay "masterpiece." Ruben, wearing a cranberry leisure suit, stood taller than his husband, glaring at his watch. In producer mode, he offered a tactful reminder. "Nicky, hurry up before we lose the light!"

"I feel like we're in bed on the first Saturday night of the month," Martin replied to his husband, scratching his bald head.

With Barclay's costume malfunction thankfully solved by our costumer sewing tiny weights into the hem of Barclay's kilt, we were ready to resume shooting. I nodded to Lairie Naughton, and her large azure eyes came alive. Our makeup artist had aged the girl from a fourteen-year-old lass to a fourteen-year-old streetwalker. She was dressed in her maid's costume: a ruffled white blouse, scarlet vest and matching ankle-length skirt, chocolate-colored shawl, and leather ghillies tied above the ankles. The girl excitedly took her mark next to Barclay on the cliff's edge.

"Roll sound, camera speed, slate, background action." *I love saying that!*

Ruban ran a liver-spotted hand through his salt-and-pepper hair. "We can't afford background players in this film, Nicky. So move on. As the Scottish ancestors said, 'Head down, arse up.'"

As I often say to Noah.

"Action!"

Barclay, as his ancestor Ainsley, ran his strong thick hand through Lairie's long golden hair. "Ye are a might pretty sight, lass."

She giggled and ran away, beckoning him with her gaze to follow. Barclay obliged until his wife Moira, as Fiona Conall, blocked his path. She was dressed in the same style as Lairie; however, the wool in her outfit seemed more expensive. "So ye have been dipping ye finger into the new batter, have ye, Ainsley. And the maid's so thin she doesn't have enough room inside her for a rheumatic pain." Suddenly, the right side of Moira's face drooped.

"Cut! Make-up for Moira, Maureen!" *Try saying that three times fast.*

As a young actress, Moira Dunn had done some theatre, television commercials, and daytime drama. When she hit thirty, the work dried up. So she applied for a job at Conall Castle and became the desk clerk — and Mrs. Barclay Conall, mistress of Conall Castle. Making her comeback in our film at thirty-six caused the actress to employ an old acting trick: using an elastic headband to stretch her face up under a wig for a temporary face lift. However, when a tree branch caught on the wig, Moira's face fell faster than the economy after the Republicans' bank deregulation.

Noah placed a reassuring hand on my shoulder. "The scene looks good, Nicky. And the countryside is gorgeous."

"Like you." I kissed his cheek. "And you did a great job coaching the amateur actors." I ran my hands through his velvety golden locks and smelled a field of strawberries. "Are you sorry we came to Scotland?"

"I'm happy to be wherever you are." He hugged my neck.

With her face now tauter than a rubber band around a

politician's benefits package, Moira resumed her position. I said, "Let's pick up from where we left off for Take Two." I called out my usual director's jargon.

Barclay's face turned as red as his kilt. "Nonsense! Ye bum's out the windie, Fiona." He laughed wickedly. "And *ye* are the wee hen who never layed an egg, aren't ye, temptress?" He yanked on his wife's long auburn hair, and Maya blue eyes bulged out of her head. So did her hair extension. "Cut!"

After Moira's hair was repaired, we moved on for Take Three. Barclay shouted, "I know ye and me middle brother have been laying heather down in the fields, Fiona."

She clutched the broach at her chest. "Ye are all bum and parsley, Ainsley."

That's like our classy American expression, "You're full of dog-doody."

Magnus Conall, as Archibald Conall, came out from behind a boulder. Dressed in the same manner as his older brother, he tripped over his cloak. "Cut!"

For Take Four, Magnus stood between his brother and sister-in-law. Except for his wide nose and shorter height, you could hardly tell the two brothers apart.

Barclay spit in his brother's face. "Ye have been lying with me wife!"

"No! All ye eggs are double-yoked, brother."

That's Scottish for "nutty as a fruitcake." No pun intended.

I whispered to Noah, "Either you're a terrific acting coach, or Cain and Abel have some competition with the Conall brothers."

Magnus yanked Barclay's sporran from its chain. "Ye are not fit to wear the family crest and rule the castle." The veins in his neck bulged. "Or to lie with a woman like Fiona!"

Barclay rushed Magnus and (thanks to Noah's fight choreography) wrestled him to the ground. The two men rolled over each other, until they approached the lip of the cliff, where Magnus dangled Barclay over the edge (with a hidden platform we built beneath him).

"Tatties over the side, brother."

"Lad, help me up!" Barclay called out.

Magnus laughed wickedly. "A clean shirt will do ye, brother, as ye go to your grave."

Horror filled Barclay's face. "I am doomed. They have thrown a stone at my door!"

Moira stood above her husband defiantly. "Ye are Black Donald's now, husband. To Hell with you!"

"Cut"

Our boom microphone operator helped Barclay to his feet. Next, our prop mistress placed a dummy of Barclay in the same spot. I gave the signal and the camera operator filmed the dummy, as Barclay, falling over the edge of the cliff into the pounding waves below.

Martin applauded wildly and wept. "My masterpiece is finally brought to life! And the Academy Award for Best Screenplay goes to Martin Anderson!"

"You have a better chance of winning The Miss America Pageant," Ruben retorted.

We shot the scene again from various angles, and yet again with close-ups on the three actors. When we finished before dark, Ruben sighed in relief. Our crew packed up the equipment into the truck. The rest of us boarded the van. As we rode to the castle, I held Noah's hand and gazed out the window. The violet and amber rolling hills were surrounded by the foamy sea. The lighthouse stood majestically in the distance.

Noah squeezed my hand. "It's so beautiful and magical. I can't believe we're really here."

I squeezed back. "And we're living in a castle! I feel like a king." *Or a queen.*

"I always feel like a king when I'm with you." Noah kissed my sideburn.

As the van passed the old abandoned abbey and approached Conall Castle, I felt like an eighteenth century

Scottish lord. The crystal-blue lake weaved grandly around the two hundred acres. A long white stone bridge led to the three-story, one-hundred-room, white stone castle with four turrets, eighty stone fireplaces, thirty stained-glass windows, and Scotland's national flag with a white cross and blue background flying proudly at the entrance.

Our driver dropped us off, and Noah and I walked across the bridge, giggling at the moat underneath us, and made our way to the massive beechwood door to the entrance.

Barclay Conall led us into the vast hallway as he admired the Conall coat of arms flanked on the wall by large ornate pewter sconces. At the sight of the knight in shining armor, I saluted, and Noah whistled, "If I Only Had a Heart."

Then the lord of the castle stood at the enormous stone fireplace opposite the front reception desk. "Dinner is in fifteen minutes in the Great Hall."

Everyone scattered down the long hallway filled with medieval leather benches, chairs, end tables, chests, and heavy gold-framed pictures of Conall ancestors throughout the centuries. I noticed that Moira walked with Barclay's middle brother, Magnus, rather than with her husband.

Noah and I made our way up the gigantic poplar wood staircase. After standing all day and evening, the thick burgundy carpet on the steps was a welcome cushion to my tired feet. Noah admired the intricate molding of lions in various positions on the staircase, walls, and pewter chandelier above us. "Nicky, the castle must be much more crowded when open for business."

"I prefer having it to ourselves." I pinched his firm bottom and he giggled.

On the second floor, Noah and I headed down the long corridor and knocked on Mom and Dad's door. Dad opened it, wearing a T-shirt and Bermuda shorts.

"Dad, we're in Scotland, not the Caribbean," Noah said.

"A vacation's a vacation." Dad welcomed us into his room. "This is some place, huh?" He gestured to the large canopy bed. "And look at that!" Poking my arm, he added, "You planning on giving it to Noah in the caboose tonight?"

Noah turned scarlet.

Dad laughed uproariously. "How are my two boys?"

"Tired." I sat on an ornate bench.

"Stay and watch TV with me." Dad opened a giant oak wardrobe revealing a flat screen television.

Did they have those in the eighteenth century?

He sat next to me and ran a hand over his bald head. "*Braveheart* is on tonight."

Noah sat on a wide oak chair opposite us. "Dad, you're in Scotland. Why not do some sightseeing?"

"No sights can beat the locations in *Braveheart*," Dad said.

The door opened, and an iPhone covered my face. "What a cute picture of you two boys. Do you like my new iPhone?" Mom texted and then smiled proudly. "Judy from Wisconsin says her son and son-in-law, Tommy and Timmy, have never been to Scotland."

Dad laughed. "Lucky for Jack. He'd have gotten stuck with the bill."

"How are my boys?" Mom kissed every inch of our faces.

I wiped Mom's tangerine lipstick off with a handkerchief. "How are Tommy and Timmy?"

"They're worried about their little adopted daughter from Vietnam. Poor Dung gets under everyone's feet, and Judy and her husband Jack keep stepping on Dung!" Mom sat on the canopy bed and adjusted the tie of her tangerine robe. "I think Tommy and Timmy are spreading Dung too thin with baby classes in sign language, swimming, and art."

"All paid for by Grandpa Jack," Dad added.

Mom patted her dyed blonde hair into place. "Dung is a sweet child, but no kid is as gifted and talented as our grandson."

"Amen," Dad said while readying the television remote control.

"Speaking of Taavi." Noah looked around the room. "Where is he?"

Always the actor, our son entered from the bathroom on cue.

Mom sat Taavi next to her on the bed and draped an arm around him.

Wearing a canary polo shirt that highlighted his olive-colored skin and black hair, Taavi looked adorable with his legs dangling off the high bed. "Grandma and I explored the castle." His dimples appeared. "I found a secret passageway."

"A sleuth, like your dads," Dad said.

"And like your grandfather," Mom added.

Taavi wiped his palms on his sky-blue shorts. "I can't wait to shoot my scenes."

Noah smiled. "Will you steal them from me?"

"That's the plan." Taavi offered his father a hang loose sign and a huge grin.

Mom said, "Judy was very impressed with our little Taavi's acting in that slasher film you all did last year."

"As she should be," Dad said as if he were Taavi's agent.

"Judy said that little Dung's chocolate coloring would show up well on film."

"Too bad Tommy and Timmy aren't in the movie business like our Nicky and Noah," Dad said.

Mom and Dad laughed together triumphantly.

I noticed a gold necklace around Dad's neck as it danced over his flabby chest. "I've never seen that before,

Dad."

He stuck out his already protruding stomach. "What, my sexy physique?" Dad winked at Noah. "I may be giving you a run for your money tonight, Noah."

Noah's scarlet cheeks turned crimson.

I walked over to Dad. "I mean your necklace."

"He's worn that thing around his neck since I met him," Mom said.

Taking it in my hand, I admired the fine craftsmanship of the gold two-leaf clover.

"It's really a four-leaf clover," Dad explained, "but the other two leaves broke off."

"Where did you get it?"

"In a little shop on a glen in a valley in the highlands of Scotland. A year before I met Mom, I visited the land of my ancestors to find my roots."

"While I was covering up mine with peroxide," Mom said with a smile.

"But my ancestors didn't come from a place like this." Dad explained, "They were sheepherders." The dairy farmer added, "Milking is in my blood."

"So is high cholesterol from all the cheese he eats," Mom said as if speaking about a death row criminal.

Dad patted his stomach. "I like food."

"Me too, Grandpa." Taavi patted his stomach too.

"Did you all eat dinner?" Noah asked with concern showing on his handsome face.

Mom nodded. "A sweet young waiter named Donal served us in the dining room." She giggled like a young girl. "He paid extra attention to *me*."

"Were you jealous?" I asked Dad.

He waved me away like a color guard on speed. "Donal was a nice-looking guy. But he reminded me of you and Noah, if you know what I mean."

My father-in-law developed gaydar?

Taavi's dark eyes glistened in delight. "We ate cock-adoodle-doo soup, blood pudding, green fish, and bread for short people."

As if a United Nations translator, Mom said, "Taavi means cock-a-leekie soup—"

Okay, it's not what you're thinking. It's a soup with chicken, bacon, leeks, and spices.

Mom continued, "—black pudding—"

Get ready to be grossed out. It's pork fat, pork blood, oatmeal, and oat and barley groats.

"—scallops with cabbage and green apple sauce, and shortbread."

"I texted all my friends from school. I can't believe we're living in a real castle!"

Noah rose and took Taavi's hand. "Let's get you into bed now, young man."

"Can't I stay up and watch a movie with Grandpa?"

"Actors need their rest." I took Taavi's other hand. "Mom, Dad, we'll see you both tomorrow."

Mom took more pictures and then texted. "Judy says even with her photo gallery full of Dung, you are the most handsome family she knows."

I blew a kiss to Mom. Noah, Taavi, and I said "goodnight" and then walked to the next room. After Taavi changed into his T-shirt and boxers, he jumped into his high canopy bed. Noah placed the white silk sheet over him and sat on one side, while I rested on the other. The towering dark oak headboard hovered over him as if protecting our son from any harm.

"Are you happy we're here?" I asked.

Taavi nodded. "Scotland is really cool. And I like being with you, Dad, Grandma, and Grandpa."

Noah moved the hair off his forehead. "And the movie?"

"That's the best part!"

That's my son.

Taavi smiled. "Since it's my second film, will I get a

raise? Special billing?"

That's definitely my son.

Noah laughed and winked at me. "I'll speak to your agent."

I started to rise, but Taavi pulled my arm. "Pop, this week, be careful."

"What do you mean?" I asked.

He sounded more like a twenty-year-old than a ten-year-old. "You know what happens every time you direct a show."

Noah kissed his forehead. "Nothing bad will happen with the three of us together."

"If it does, can I help you investigate?" Taavi asked like a second-string baseball player begging to leave the bench.

"We're here to make a movie and have a vacation." I kissed his cheek. "Get some sleep. If you need anything while we're downstairs, Grandpa and Grandma are right next door."

"When will you be back?" Taavi asked like a Dickens character left in the coal bin.

I stood. "In about an hour."

Noah rose. "And then we'll be in the adjoining room through that door. But we will check in on you when we get upstairs."

Taavi raised himself up on one elbow. "Thanks for taking me."

"You're our son. Why wouldn't we take you on our vacation?" I asked.

"No, I mean from Hawaii," Taavi said.

Noah's eyes brimmed with tears, as he kissed Taavi's cheek. "Goodnight, son."

Noah and I left Taavi's room, walked down the hall, and knocked on Martin and Ruben's door.

My best friend and department head, Martin Anderson, opened the door and stood next to us in the hallway. Noah and I shared a smile at the long fuchsia satin robe that swam off Martin's tiny body, and the cold cream caked on his thin face.

"Are you and Ruben coming down to dinner?" I asked.

Martin replied, "A cute, young, friend-of-Dorothy waiter, Donal, brought up our meal."

Donal gets around.

Martin said, "Donal seemed to be checking me out."

"To see if you were still alive." Ruben appeared in the doorway, wearing a fuchsia nightshirt.

Ignoring his longtime husband, Martin said, "But I don't eat too much this late at night." He added like a fitness guru, "My body is a temple."

"But nobody wants to worship at it." Ruben replied.

"When I reach old age, I'll look into all those vitamins Nicky takes."

"Martin, you're well past reaching old age. You're a heartbeat away from cremation."

"And you are my partner."

They giggled and kissed.

Ruben checked his watch. "Well, it's past my bedtime."

"No it isn't, Ruben." Martin explained, "It's five hours later in Scotland than in the US." He smirked. "So it's only afternoon, our time."

"The perfect time for a mid-day nap." Ruben turned to Martin like a lost boy. "Aren't you going to tuck me in?"

Martin raised his dark eyes to the chandelier. "In a minute."

"Nicky, we shoot bright and early tomorrow morning. Get some sleep." Our producer added, "If it means locking Noah in the dungeon."

After Ruben had gone back into their room, Martin whispered, "Well?"

"Well what?" I asked.

He looked both ways as if foreign spies might be listening. "Tell me all about the Conalls."

"The first day of shooting went well," I replied.

Martin said with the patience of a customer service clerk at five p.m., "You know what I mean, Nicky."

Ruben opened the door. "You'd better give him the gossip, Nicky, or I'll never get to sleep."

After Ruben closed the door, I said, "You may have ESP, Martin."

"What do you mean?" He turned to Noah. "What does he mean?"

Noah explained, "As in your film adaptation of Barclay Conall's novel with Ainsley and Fiona, there seems to be some strain in Barclay and Moira's marriage."

"I knew it!" Martin jumped up and down like a rabbit in a mine field. "'Down-on-her-luck actress Moira Dunn married the eldest Conall brother to be mistress of Conall Castle, but her untrue blue eyes are on macho middle brother, money-man Magnus." *Try saying that three times fast.*

"We don't know that for sure."

"Then find out! And get the story on cute little Donal too—tonight at dinner." Martin added like a general talking to his privates (no pun intended), "Find out who's getting made in the misty moors—and report back!"

Having been given our assignments, Noah and I wished Martin pleasant dreams, and then we headed down the stairs to the Great Hall.

The gigantic room was crowned by an enormous bronze chandelier hovering over numerous large wooden tables. Our cast of characters (pun intended) had changed into jeans and flannel shirts and were seated at a large table opposite a sprawling stone fireplace with the Conall coat of arms proudly displayed on its mantel. Noah and I took the two empty chairs at one end. At the head of the table sat the lord of the manor, Barclay Conall. Barclay's wife, Moira, was next, with Barclay's middle brother, Magnus, following. Young Lairie Naughton from Housekeeping sat at Noah's side.

Since nobody was speaking to each other, and we weren't having a séance, I cleared my throat. "I'm pleased with our work today, everyone."

"It felt so good to be back in front of the camera!" Moira flicked back her long red hair and batted her long lashes in my direction. "Thank you, Mr. Director."

Barclay glared at his wife. "It has to be on the page before it can be on the stage."

"And you are always center stage, brother." Magnus rubbed his wide nose.

Barclay's eyes turned greener. "Have you forgotten that *I* wrote the original book, Magnus?"

"No. And I also haven't forgotten that *you* inherited the castle." Magnus's broad shoulders tightened.

"I inherited Conall Castle because I'm firstborn."

"Which you never let us forget."

"Sour grapes aren't on the menu tonight, Magnus. And since we're talking about forgetting. You haven't done the monthly audit of the books." Barclay feigned forgetfulness. "Oh, that's right, you didn't do it last month either."

Moira said quickly, "It was busy behind the front desk last week."

"I'm sure it was *very* busy behind the front desk." Barclay glared at Moira and Magnus.

Her fists clenched. "I'm guessing it was as busy as *you* were in Housekeeping with Brody Naughton!"

The three Conalls glanced at each other like cowboys itching to be the first to draw their guns. *Why do I feel like the host of a reality TV show?* I changed the subject. "How does everyone like Martin's screenplay?"

Moira replied, "Sex and violence sells. My local psychic told me the film is going to be a big hit."

"Of course you like it, Moira. I die in the first scene." Barclay ran a thick hand through this thick auburn hair as he drank some ale.

"Which was fun to do," Magnus said with a smirk.

Lairie giggled. "It wasn't too hard playing a maid, since I *am* a maid. But I loved every minute of it!"

Barclay snapped at her, "Careful, Lairie. You'll become an actress like Moira. And when you get old, the offers will stop coming."

A small young man with striking blue eyes, shining blond hair, and a milk-and-honey complexion served the cock-a-leekie soup from the large buffet against the wall.

Lairie's face lit up. "Hi, Donal."

He winked at her. "I'm honored to serve such a famous actress."

Donal served Noah and me last, and everyone ate their soup. I remembered Martin's order. "Donal, you're quite popular with my family and friends upstairs."

"It was my pleasure to serve them." The square-shouldered young waiter, appropriately wearing a white shirt and black pants, offered a firm handshake to Noah and me. "I'm Donal Blair."

"Nicky Abbondanza."

"And Nicky's husband and colleague, Noah Oliver."

"Donal's my friend," Lairie said.

"Then he must be a good man," Noah replied.

"Lairie, what are you doing up so late?" A tall, handsome man with long blond hair and a matching beard entered and stood above the girl.

Donal replied, "Lairie just returned from the film shoot on the moors."

"This is between my daughter and me, Donal," he said.

"Dad, Donal was just—"

"I know what Donal was doing. And he should stick to serving the soup."

"Lairie has to eat dinner, Brody," Donal replied.

"She's *my* daughter. I'll decide when she needs to eat," Brody said.

Donal's eyes filled with tears. "I was just trying to

help."

"Don't!"

Donal hurried out of the room.

Is that regret in Brody's blue eyes?

Barclay picked up his soup bowl to drink the last few drops, and then wiped his mouth with his sleeve. "You gave your permission for Lairie to be in the movie, Brody."

"I gave my permission for a lot of things that I later regretted, Barclay."

"I know the feeling." Barclay sneered at him.

Magnus and Moira shared a telling glance.

Barclay asked Brody, "Don't you have housekeeping duties to do?"

Brody replied, "I want to make sure Lairie is all right."

Lairie rose. "Dad, it was so amazing being in the movie!"

His face softened. "I'm glad, honey."

"After I finish dinner, I'll come up and tell you all about it."

Brody placed a gentle hand on his daughter's cheek. "Sure, honey."

Barclay said, "Now go back to cleaning the sheets, Brody, or whatever you were doing."

Lairie's eyes thinned. "There's no reason to be rude. My father was concerned about me."

"Watch your tongue, lass."

Brody's nostrils flared. "Don't talk to my daughter like that, Barclay!"

"This is *my* castle. I'll speak however I like!"

Donal entered with the next course.

Brody said, "Donal—"

"I'm busy. I have to serve dinner." Donal rushed past him.

Brody growled and then stormed out.

Barclay rose.

"Leave it alone, Barclay," Moira said.

"I left it alone a long time ago." Barclay sat and lifted his fork. "Let's eat and go to bed."

Magnus smiled devilishly at Moira. "That sounds good to me."

"I'm not surprised," Barclay said.

After I finished dinner, I swallowed my vitamins with a sip of ale.

Lairie pointed to one of them. "What's that one?"

"Milk thistle. I read somewhere that it's supposed to be good for your liver." *Ironic that I just drank it with alcohol.*

After dinner, Noah and I climbed the long staircase, checked in on Taavi who was sleeping soundly, and went to our room. We stripped to our T-shirts and shorts faster than a priest meeting an altar boy in the church supply closet. Then we leapt (literally) into the enormous bed and rested our backs on the tall oak headboard. I wrapped my arm around Noah's smooth shoulder, and we shared a strawberry-scented kiss. Then I said, "Taavi was right. Blood pudding *was* on the castle menu tonight."

Noah kissed the cleft in my chin and then rested his head on my chest. "The Conalls certainly aren't one big happy family."

I said, "I think Moira is cheating on Barclay with his brother Magnus. And did you see the sexual tension between Barclay and Brody from Housekeeping?"

"It was as palpable as the tension between Brody and Donal, the waiter."

"True. I'd like to cast Brody as Prince Bruce in our movie, and Donal as Older Roddy."

"Speaking of our cast of characters, where was the youngest brother, the restaurant manager, Fergus? Barclay said Fergus is engaged to one of the waiters."

We looked at each other and burst out laughing.

"When did we start channeling Martin and Ruben?" I asked.

"Ever since we've become an old married couple

tucked away in a castle." Noah kissed my sideburn.

Gazing around the room at the huge wardrobe, stone fireplace, and tall stained-glass windows, I said, "I feel like the lord of the castle."

Noah giggled. "What does that make *me*?"

I squeezed him in closer. "The lord's squeeze."

We shared a long, wet kiss.

Noah said, "Shouldn't we get some sleep? We have an early morning shoot."

"We have a late-night shoot too." I nibbled on his earlobes. "In a castle or a hovel, you're the only man for me, Noah."

We kissed again.

"You make me so happy, Nicky."

"You ain't seen nothin' yet." I lowered Noah onto his back and lay on top of him. As he massaged my back, I kissed his eyes, nose, and sweet lips. He cried out in delight when I pinched his nipples. After I flexed my biceps, Noah kissed them and then squeezed my pectoral muscles. Next, he kissed the palms of my hands and then rested them on his buttocks. I squeezed his bottom as we kissed. "I want you so much, Noah."

"You've got every part of me, including my heart."

We slid into the sixty-nine position. Noah licked my abdominal muscles as I kissed the blond hair around his navel and below. In turn, Noah tugged at my pubic hair, and then ran his tongue along my ample junk. Then he kissed my mushroom head again and again.

After we both let out a satisfied moan, I took Noah's long, thin, curved manhood into my mouth. He stretched his mouth open and did the same for me. We both sucked slowly and gently, like members of a symphony orchestra in perfect rhythm.

"I want you inside me, Nicky."

"Always." I kneeled at Noah's waist, and gently pushed him down onto his back. Then I pressed Noah's legs back, kissed the soft soles of his feet, and licked his warm toes. I lowered his legs over my back and entered him slowly. Noah grabbed my thighs and pulled them in closer with a grateful sigh. Then I grasped his tool, rubbing and thrusting until our passion exploded amidst cries of ecstasy.

I whispered in Noah's ear what was in my heart, "You are all I ever wanted."

"You're mine forever."

As we lay in each other's arms, Noah snored softly. Suddenly, a feeling of doom overtook me—a premonition that murder would veer its head at Conall Castle, and Noah, Taavi, and I would very soon be in grave danger!

CHAPTER TWO

I woke jet-lagged the next morning to Noah acting as cheery as an anti-gay politician at a gay orgy during a blackout. He smothered my yawning face and droopy eyes with kisses, helped me out of bed like a nursing home aide, and gently pushed me into the (thankfully) modernized bathroom. After I showered and dressed, Noah and I met up with Taavi, Mom, Dad, Martin, and Ruben in the hallway, and we all made our way down the long staircase.

Looking peachy in a peach sundress, Mom took pictures with her iPhone for Judy in Wisconsin. After nearly tripping while texting, she said, "Judy wishes Tommy and Timmy would take her to a fancy place like this."

Dad laughed. "They'd have to borrow money from Jack."

Mom added, "She said if little Dung were here, Dung would plop down on a bench until they scooped her off."

Looking out of place in a loud Hawaiian shirt and Bermuda shorts, Dad scanned the television listings in his hand. "*Rob Roy* is on in an hour. I hope breakfast doesn't take too long."

"It won't," Ruben said with a glance at his watch.

Mom raised her eyes to the intricate lion molding on the ceiling. "Dad, we're in Scotland. Don't you want to see the countryside?"

"I'll see plenty of Scottish countryside in *Rob Roy*," Dad replied.

We were greeted at the Great Hall's entrance by Fergus Conall, the youngest and smallest Conall brother. The dark circles under his glazed-over hazel eyes caused him to look older than his twenty-five years. Conall Castle's restaurant manager said, "Welcome to breakfast."

The Sherlock Holmes in me noticed the smell of liquor on his breath and the wrinkles in his dark suit.

Fergus placed his shaking hand on another young man's elbow. "Hamish will serve you breakfast."

"Good." Dad patted his protruding stomach. "What's on the menu?"

Hamish replied, "Goat's milk, farmhouse eggs, and lorne sausage with black bread and butter."

Dad led Mom and Taavi to our table.

Since I hadn't met the morning waiter, I offered Hamish my hand. "Nicky Abbondanza."

Wearing a white shirt and black pants, the tall man shook my hand. "Hamish MacAlastair."

Fergus said, "Hamish is my best waiter." He blew a kiss at Hamish. "And my fiancé."

"Congratulations!" Noah shook their hands. "I'm Noah Oliver, Nicky's husband and partner in crime solving. When's the big day?"

Fergus grimaced. "As soon as I can talk Barclay into opening the ballroom."

"The ballroom?" Ruben asked, always scouting for new film locations.

"It's at the far end of this wing." Fergus pointed his long nose in that direction.

Hamish explained, "I have my heart set on us marrying there. But due to its immense size and antique furnishings, Barclay keeps it locked."

"And it will stay locked." Barclay entered looking like the laird of the castle in a turquoise dress shirt, black vest, and black dress slacks.

"Like my father who ran Conall Castle before him, my

brother is somewhat of a skinflint," Fergus said.

Barclay stared down his youngest brother. "With the drop in hotel revenues, we can't afford to waste money on frivolity."

Fergus's temper flared as red as his hair. "I didn't realize my wedding was a 'frivolity.'"

"Well, now you know," Barclay said.

Always concerned for others, Noah asked, "Has the hotel business hit a snag?"

Barclay replied, "Business is better than ever. But our cash flow isn't."

"And my brother is convinced it's *my* fault." Magnus entered in his kilt costume for the day's shooting.

"Excuse us." In his canary leisure suit with matching watch, Ruben ushered Noah and me to our table.

In a canary bowtie and sweater vest, Martin said to me sotto voce, "The three Conall brothers seem to get along as badly as priests and reluctant altar boys."

Moira entered in her film costume. She met up with Magnus, and they whispered together near the buffet.

Martin stared at me with his mouth open, as if ready to catch flies. "Tell me what you know, Nicky!"

"You better do it, Nicky, or he'll die of old age tonight and haunt you," said Ruben.

I explained, "Moira and Magnus seem to have a... connection."

Hamish served breakfast and then left our table. My jealous bone emerged as Noah never took his eyes off Hamish. I breathed a sigh of relief when Noah said to me, "Hamish would make a good Prince Jock in our movie."

"Good casting, Noah. I never asked Brody and Donal if they'd play the roles I selected for them."

"I'll take care of it."

Lairie Naughton, wearing her Aggie the maid costume, strode in and stood before us. "Good morning." The girl giggled. "I can't wait to die in my scene!"

That caught Taavi's attention, as did Lairie. "You get to die?"

She nodded. "Isn't that totally amazing?"

"Totally!"

My ten-year-old son seemed to age four years. Looking adorable, or should I say "handsome" in his violet polo shirt and tan shorts, Taavi smiled at Lairie. "How do you die?"

Lairie replied as excitedly as a conservative politician giving a tax cut to a huge corporation, "I get thrown into the lake! I texted my friends at school about it. They were already jealous since I got to take off the last week of school to be in the movie."

Taavi pulled on my arm. "Pop, can I go to the shoot today?"

"Sure," I replied.

Taavi and Lairie shared a smile.

"I invited my dad and Donal to watch too." She added conspiratorially to Taavi, "When we're through shooting, I can show you some secret places around the castle."

Taavi looked at me. After I nodded, he replied, "I'd really like that!"

"I like to pretend I'm the owner of the castle," Lairie said.

"Sounds like fun," my son the actor replied.

"It's enchanting," the fourteen-year-old said like the mistress of Conall Castle.

Noah poked Taavi's shoulder. "You can write that word on your vocabulary pad for us to go over tonight before bed."

Taavi laughed like a spelling bee champ. "I think I'm too old for that now, Dad."

Brody Naughton appeared next to his daughter. "Lairie, let the guests eat their breakfast in peace."

"We're all enjoying Lairie's company." *Especially Taavi.*

Upon seeing him, Mom asked the head of

Housekeeping, "Brody, when you get a moment, can I have a second pillow?"

Noah did a double-take. "You never slept with two pillows."

Mom replied, "And I don't want to now. The pillow is to put over your father's face when he snores."

"Hey, I don't snore," Dad said, seeming offended.

Mom laughed. "Right. And I don't take pictures."

Fergus joined us. "Brody, is there a reason why you aren't in Housekeeping?"

"I was looking after my daughter," Brody replied.

"You looked. Now scurry off." The restaurant manager gestured to the door.

Brody glared down at Fergus. "I can be with whomever I like."

Fergus snickered. "That theory didn't work out so well with Barclay, now did it?"

"One day you, or one of your brothers, will push me too far," Brody said.

Lairie glared at Fergus. Then she kissed her father's cheek. "I'm fine, Dad. Why don't you visit with Donal? He's off this morning."

Fergus smirked. "Hm, I wonder why you would be visiting Donal?"

"Donal's our friend," Lairie said.

"You make trouble for Donal, Fergus, and you'll answer to *me*." Brody stormed off.

Lairie followed him. "The Conalls aren't worth your anger, Dad. They're self-centered bullies, the lot of them."

As Hamish replenished our drinks, his chestnut-colored hair flew in various directions, but his umber eyes were focused on his fiancé. "Fergus, don't you think you were a bit hard on Brody?"

Fergus pulled back his shoulders. "Actually, I don't. Now do you have any other questions for me, Hamish, or are you ready to focus on our other guests?"

Hamish gasped and then rushed off with Fergus following him.

Martin looked as if his appendix would burst. "Do you think there is something going on romantically between Barclay and Brody, or Brody and Donal?"

I shrugged.

"Well, find out!" Martin finished his hot cocoa.

I swallowed my vitamins, minerals, and milk thistle with (appropriately) a glass of milk and braced myself for the day's shooting.

We all headed out of the Great Hall and walked through the long hallway. Once outside, we crossed the stone bridge and boarded the van. All, that is, except Dad who had an appointment with Rob Roy, and Mom who ventured out to the abbey—iPhone in hand—to take pictures for Judy in Wisconsin. The crew members left first in a truck with the equipment, and our van followed.

Lairie and Taavi sat together in the back of the van sharing their passion for popular movies with special effects that gave me motion sickness. Magnus and his sister-in-law, Moira, sat next to them, running their lines for the upcoming scene...and sharing furtive glances.

The youngest Conall brother, Fergus, was in the middle section of the van whispering with his fiancé, Hamish, the morning waiter. Sitting in front of them, I couldn't help overhearing their conversation (since I stretched my neck backwards and tilted my ear in their direction).

"What time did you get back last night?" Hamish asked.

"Not too late," Fergus replied.

"I woke at three a.m. and you weren't there, Fergus."

"Are you keeping tabs on me?"

"To be honest, I am."

"Then stop."

"No, *you* stop, Fergus. Stop behaving like a spoiled

teenager."

"Hamish, if my brother wasn't so stingy, there wouldn't be a problem," Fergus said.

"You can't blame everything on Barclay," his fiancé replied.

"Aye, I can. And I do!"

Next to them sat Brody, the head of Housekeeping, and Donal, the evening waiter. "I'm looking forward to watching Lairie's scene," Donal said.

"It's all she's talked about for weeks." Brody groaned. "I hope she doesn't lose her job at the castle."

"She won't. Lairie's a good worker."

"But Barclay isn't a good boss."

"You would know more about Barclay than I, Brody."

"Are you ever going to stop throwing ancient history with Barclay and me in my face!"

Obviously hurt, Donal blurted out, "I don't blame Fenella for leaving you when Lairie was a girl. I don't blame everyone else for leaving you too!"

"My parents didn't choose to leave me, and you know it. They died in that plane crash three years ago. And Barclay didn't leave me either. We weren't a couple. I wouldn't want to be with anyone but..." Brody looked away.

Donal bit his lip. "I'm sorry."

Brody softened. "I'm sorry too."

"Maybe someday somebody won't leave you." He smiled. "If you let him in."

In the front row, Martin, Ruben, and Noah sat to my left, deeply immersed in their conversation about the subtext of the screenplay. According to Martin, the battles between the Conall family members in the script are symbolic of the Anglo-Scottish wars.

I turned to Barclay on my right. His broad shoulders were squeezed in between mine and the side of the van. "You've been a good sport about the screen adaptation veering a bit from your novel."

"A bit? That's like saying Moira's a bit star-struck." As we drove on the steep cliff, Barclay stared out the window at the azure sky rendezvousing with the cerulean sea.

"How did you lose your parents?"

"They died in a car accident off this cliff a year ago."

"I'm sorry."

His voice cracked. "Kendric and Emilia Conall. They're in the Conall graveyard on my property."

"I admire you for keeping Conall Castle all in the family."

His handsome face hardened. "You have an expression in the States, 'If you want something done right, you'd better do it yourself.' That pretty much sums up the worth of Magnus, Moira, and Fergus at Conall Castle." Barclay folded his strong arms across his wide chest. "My father knew what he was doing when he left Conall Castle to me."

"Do you and Moira have children?"

"Moira doesn't want children."

"Your staff must be of help to you."

"Donal is focused on Brody. Lairie is focused on play pretend." Barclay's biceps pressed against his shirt. "And Brody is focused on trying to get into my bed."

"We're here!" Ruben rushed us out of the van to an iridescent lake surrounded by a hunter-green meadow. As the crew set up the lights, camera, and boom microphone, Noah worked with the three actors on their actions, objectives, and emotional beats. At the same time, our wardrobe mistress checked the actors' costumes, and our makeup woman applied the makeup. I stood under the shade of a sprawling old oak tree with Taavi, Martin, and Ruben.

Martin squinted up at the golden sun rays bathing the area. "Thank goodness for this tree. I wouldn't want the sun to wrinkle my skin."

"Says the prune who thinks he's still a plum," Ruben

said.

"To the next prune in the jar," Martin retorted.

Ignoring his husband, Ruben took in a deep breath. "Thank goodness the weather is perfect again today."

"Yes. What a romantic spot." Martin took Ruben's hand.

Bending back Martin's hand to check his watch, Ruben asked, "When will you start shooting, Nicky?"

"As soon as the DP gives me the high sign," I replied.

With his own romantic notions stifled, Martin whispered in my ear, "Maybe you should welcome our visitors to the set, Nicky. Find out which Scot is girding his loins and lifting his kilt for which other Scot!"

I bent down to Taavi. "Will you be all right here with Martin and Ruben?"

"Of course he will." Martin pushed me away. "We adore this child." Then he turned to Taavi. "Now go play with the camera operator."

Mesmerized as usual by the movie equipment, Taavi "helped" our director of photography and camera operator set up the shots for our upcoming scene.

I headed over to a large rock, where the visitors stood, and said to Brody Naughton, "Your coming means a great deal to Lairie."

The head of Housekeeping scratched at his blond beard. "Lairie's all I have."

"I overheard you (*accidentally on purpose*) speaking with Donal in the van about your ex-wife."

Brody chortled. "She was a waitress at the castle. Fenella left with the bartender when Lairie was a baby."

"How tragic."

"Not really. We didn't have much of a marriage. And Fenella had no interest in being a mother."

"I'm sorry."

"Don't be. I'm not."

"And like Barclay, you lost your parents recently."

He nodded. "Three years ago, in a plane crash."

Channeling Martin, I said, "You and Barclay must be a comfort for each other."

He burst out laughing. "Hardly. Barclay doesn't comfort anyone, except himself. He wouldn't allow my parents to be buried in the Conall Castle cemetery. So they are buried in a public plot outside the castle property." He blinked back tears. "Elsbeth and Robbie Naughton. Buried like dogs."

I noticed Donal Blair nearby, waving to Lairie who excitedly returned the wave.

"It seems like you and Lairie have a devoted friend in Donal."

Brody's strong jaw tightened. "I know what you're inferring. And you're barking up the wrong Scottish pine tree."

"What am I inferring?"

"That Donal and I are lovers."

"That's none of my business."

"You're right. But since you have so many questions about Barclay, Donal, and me, I'll give you an answer. A man can't love another man."

"Are Noah and I goldfish?"

"As my father said, two men can have a sexual release, but love—no."

"My husband and I disagree with you. So do Martin and Ruben who have been together for forty years (*of squabbling*) having raised two grown daughters."

Brody rubbed his thick neck. "It's how I was brought up. In honor of my parents, I aim to stick by that."

"We love who we love. Just like your parents did. Would they want you to be alone?"

"Nobody loves me."

"Maybe you need to give others a chance." I glanced over at the sun lighting Donal's hair a burst of gold. "It's never too late to see the light, Brody."

Ruben called for quiet, and I led a rehearsal of our scene. When I was satisfied with the acting and technical elements, I stood behind the camera operator and called out, "Lights. Roll sound. Camera. Slate. Action!" *I really love doing that!*

Moira (as Fiona) and Magnus (as her brother-in-law Archibald) kissed on the meadow. When they parted, the large brooch at her chest caught on Magnus's tunic.

"Cut!"

As our costumer separated them, I glanced over to the viewers on the rock and noticed Barclay gritting his teeth.

When everyone was ready for Take Two, the couple, having thrown Barclay (Ainsley) off the cliff into the sea in the previous scene, fantasized about being laird and lady of Conall Castle.

Lairie (as Aggie the maid) entered the shot. "I were watching ye. And I saw what ye two did to the laird."

Magnus winced. "Don't be a wee clipe, lassie."

"I'll tattle, all right. Try and stop me."

Magnus moved toward her.

Moira held him back by grabbing his sporran chain. When he wriggled free, the chain snapped into his groin.

"Agh!"

"Cut!"

While Magnus regrouped (literally) in his kilt, I scanned the guests again and noticed Brody Naughton shooting dagger eyes at Barclay Conall.

When we shot again, Lairie cried out, "Because I luved the master."

Moira laughed wickedly, and the left side of her face fell.

"Cut!"

When Moira was pulled up tighter than a woman's girdle on the first date, in Take Four Moira called out to Lairie, "A pretty young face like yours suits the dish cloth, lassie. Stay there!"

Lairie, quite the little actress with tears brimming in her eyes and her face filled with pain, cried out, "I won't. I'll tell everyone what ye did!"

"I'll skelp yer wee behind."

Moira held Magnus's strong arm. "She's just up to high doh. I'll bring her down a peg." The older woman took a few more steps toward Lairie. Since Moira's tight face was incapable of registering an emotion, the actress squinted her eyes and wracked her body to portray her rage and venom.

Lairie screamed as Moira wrapped her hands around the girl's throat. "I've always hated ye, ye old witch!"

"To the loch with ye!" À la *Dynasty*, the two women wrestled at the water's edge. Then Moira threw Lairie into the lake and held the girl's head under the water.

Either they're both terrific actresses or they despise each other. "Cut!"

A crew member helped Lairie out of the water. As the onlookers applauded, Lairie stood on the meadow with water dripping from her long blonde hair, blouse, vest, shawl, and skirt. She bowed deeply, enjoying the accolades.

Taavi called out, "Bravo!"

Lairie blew him a kiss.

Noah appeared at my side.

"We created another young drama monster, Noah."

"And we wouldn't have it any other way."

We shared a quick kiss.

After our costumer dried off Lairie, we repeated the scene in close-up on Magnus, and then Moira, and finally on Lairie. By the end of the shooting, Lairie was water-logged but ecstatic. She ran toward her father who enveloped her in a huge hug. She embraced Donal next. Noticing Barclay wasn't with the other onlookers, I searched around the vicinity and couldn't spot the laird of the castle.

As it was afternoon, I called for lunch. The crew packed the equipment into the truck as the actors and spectators headed to the van. I peered over the cliff into the sea, where I spotted Barclay Conall's lifeless body on the rocks. *A Scotch on the rocks.*

CHAPTER THREE

An hour later, we were all in a castle sitting room with huge windows overlooking a running brook dancing through the meadow. Noah, Taavi, Martin, Ruben, and I rested on a circular red velvet window seat housed inside a turret. To our right, Moira Conall and her brother-in-law, Magnus Conall, occupied a Medieval-style carved oak bench. To our left, head of Housekeeping Brody Naughton, his daughter Laurie, and the evening waiter, Donal Blair, sat on a long leather sofa. Next to them, youngest brother Fergus Conall and his fiancé and morning waiter, Hamish MacAlastair, were perched on tall oak chairs.

A brawny man of about thirty years old with russet hair and matching eyes stood in front of the enormous stone fireplace at the center of the room. His dark suit was a size too small, his shoes were scuffed, and his hair was unkempt. "I am Chief Inspector Lennox Frazier of the Police Service of Scotland."

A tall, rail thin young man with carrot hair and high cheekbones stood next to him in a suit that hung off his body. "Since some of you are from the States, I'll tell you that the Chief Inspector is very high up on the ladder here. Not as high as Chief Constable Webster, but very high indeed." He looked at Frazier adoringly.

"And the Chief Constable is quite anxious for me to solve this case quickly." Frazier motioned toward the younger man. "Owen, ah rather, Inspector Steward will be assisting me with the investigation."

"Which is my pleasure." Owen blushed. "It's not my pleasure that Mr. Conall is deceased. It is my pleasure to assist Lennox. That is, the Chief Inspector."

Frazier turned toward Moira. "Our condolences for your loss, Mrs. Conall."

Moira looked about as upset as a lottery winner. "Thank you, Chief Inspector."

Frazier nodded. "Owen, rather Inspector Steward, and I interviewed and released the film crew. Given the unfortunate circumstances, I assume you will end production of your movie."

Martin clutched at his chest, and Ruben groaned.

Moira did a doubletake. "Why would we do that, Chief Inspector?" With all eyes on the not-so-grieving widow, Moira, now free of her headband, turned down the corners of her mouth. "While what happened to my husband is a tragedy, his biggest dream was to see his novel on the screen." She flung back her head stoically. "As difficult as it may be, it is my duty as his wife to make sure Barclay's vision becomes reality."

And that your film career doesn't take another nosedive.

Frazier leaned on the fireplace mantel and accidentally knocked off a brass urn. "Sorry."

I whispered to Noah, "I hope those aren't Barclay's ashes."

Noah choked back a giggle.

Owen replaced the urn. "No need to apologize, Lennox, I mean, Chief Inspector. It was just an accident. I myself have knocked over urns in the past."

Moira asked, "When will you release my husband's body, Chief Inspector?"

Magnus slid to the edge of the bench. "It's our custom to bury family members in the Conall Castle cemetery."

Brody sneered. "But only family members. Not employees. Especially in Housekeeping."

"Your mother was a maid, Brody, not a Conall,"

Magnus answered.

"Which you Conalls never let her forget." Brody folded his strong arms over his wide chest. "She died with my dad on that plane, heading for the first vacation you Conalls ever let her take."

"Then maybe she shouldn't have taken it."

Frazier scratched his stomach. "We'll release the body after forensic testing."

"Meaning the application of scientific and medical techniques to determine if there might have been foul play," Owen explained with a proud glance at Frazier.

Martin whispered in my ear, "You and Noah are here. How could there *not* have been foul play?"

I whispered back, "With a fall that long into the ocean, forensic evidence won't be of much use."

Frazier accidentally kicked over a fireplace poker. "Sorry again. I've a wee case of butterfingers."

Owen said, "That's to be expected in a place like this, Lennox, rather Chief Inspector."

As he replaced the poker, the Chief Inspector said, "It is completely possible that Mr. Conall took a nasty fall off that cliff into the sea, and there was no foul play. But we would like to speak with each of you privately."

"Just to make sure the Chief Inspector has all the information about what happened here," Owen added. "Which we will use as evidence should, on the off chance, we find out Mr. Conall died of suspicious causes." Owen sniffed proudly. "The forensic testing and your statements will assist the Chief Inspector in determining that, as only *he* can."

Frazier struggled to release a pad and pen from his suit jacket pocket and banged his elbow into a vase. "Sorry."

Owen retrieved the vase from the floor and replaced it on an end table. "No harm done, Lennox, I mean Chief Inspector. Vases often topple over in places like this."

"Owen, rather Inspector Steward, will call each of you

into the library one at a time," Frazier said.

"How long will this take," Fergus asked, glancing at his watch.

Hamish grimaced next to his fiancé. "Why? Do you have plans, Fergus?"

"I'd like to eat some lunch," the youngest brother said. *And to have a drink no doubt.*

Frazier said, "You should all be through in about an hour."

"Because the Chief Inspector is thorough, but efficient," Owen explained.

Brody placed his strong arm around Lairie's shoulder. "I don't want my daughter involved in this."

"It's all right, Dad." Lairie and Taavi exchanged conspiratorial glances, clearly excited by the possibility of a murder.

Ruben rose from his seat. "Excuse me, Chief Inspector. We have with us a famous amateur detective from America, Associate Professor Nicky Abbondanza from Treemeadow College in Vermont. If I were you, I'd enlist his help in solving the case."

I feigned modesty. "Thank you, Ruben. I only solved five mass murder cases spanning three states." Offering my most dazzling smile, I added, "When the local detectives were unable to do so."

Noah picked up his cue. "And as Holmes had his Watson, I assisted my husband in his crime-solving on each case."

"I wanted to help, but my Pop wouldn't let me," Taavi said, having been bitten by the whodunit bug.

Frazier waved his pad at me, which accidentally spun across the room into a wall clock. As Owen retrieved it, Frazier said, "Nicky Abbondanza, I read about you in a criminal justice journal."

"I'm sure whatever the article said about me was blown out of proportion...just a tad. But maybe not." I stood and offered my best profile. "I would be most happy to address the local members of the press and share insider information about each of those past cases."

Noah leapt from his seat next to me. "And since I was with Nicky every step of the way, I would be willing to fill in anything Nicky forgets to mention."

"I led Dad to find Pop at the end of the last two cases," Taavi added, slicking back his hair for the news camera.

Unleashing a row of yellow teeth, Frazier replied, "We don't have press at the northern tip of Scotland. But I would be honored if you'd join me in the interviews, Professor Abbondanza."

I found my light (from the bronze gothic chandelier above me). "I am honored to take the case...I mean assist you, Chief Inspector."

Minutes later, Frazier and I sat on high back leather chairs behind a rectangular wooden desk in the castle library. Glancing at the dusty books on bookcases and the long brocade curtains over the enormous windows, I unleashed a loud sneeze.

"Dia linn." Frazier explained, "It means 'God with us.' My dad used to say it whenever someone sneezed." He sat back with a smile. "That's Balloch Frazier, Chief Superintendent." His face saddened. "Until he died of a heart attack a few years back."

"I'm sorry." *So, nepotism explains how Frazier became Chief Inspector.*

Owen brought in Moira Conall and directed her to sit in the chair opposite us. "Please don't feel as if this is a police interrogation, Mrs. Conall." Owen's Adam's Apple bobbed up and down like a hooker in the back room of a bachelor party. "Lennox, that is Chief Inspector Frazier, is going to ask you some questions. You are not in a court of law." He looked around the room. "Though this room has a wee bit of a courtroom feel about it with the tall ceilings and wood everywhere. I'm ready, Lennox, agh, Chief

Inspector."

Frazier motioned for Owen to leave the library, and in doing so knocked over a pencil holder on the desk, which crashed into a desk clock, which toppled over onto a framed photograph of Kendric and Emilia Conall. He caught it before it went smashing to the floor. "Such a tragedy when your husband's parents had that nasty car accident off the cliff a year ago, Mrs. Conall."

Moira replied with a cool glance, "We were all devastated."

As he righted the picture, Frazier added, "It seems like I nearly just pitched them off again, didn't I?" He chuckled.

"What is it you'd like to ask me, Chief Inspector? I need to get to my room and take off this costume."

"Right! From the movie. How is that coming along?" he asked.

"Fine. Until my husband toppled off the cliff into the sea." Moira turned to me for help.

I took on the familiar role of detective. "Moira, when was the last time you saw your husband alive?"

"Right after we finished shooting the last scene. He was with the others watching from the large rock. After you called 'Cut,' everyone dispersed in different directions—like ants after a spraying."

So any of them could have done it.

Frazier attempted to write a note on his pad, but his pen was out of ink. He reached for another pen and sent the pen holder on the desk sprawling into the paper clip dispenser which spiraled into the stapler causing it to bang into the calendar and send it to the floor. "Sorry."

As Frazier bent to his knees next to me (it's not what you're thinking) to pick up the calendar, I asked Moira, "I'm guessing a child would have been of comfort to you at a time like this. Why is it that you and Barclay never had an heir to Conall Castle?"

As he stood, Frazier banged his head on the side of the

desk. "You Americans don't mince words, do you?"

"That's all right, Chief Inspector." Moira slid to the edge of her seat. "Nicky, my husband and I weren't blessed with children."

Barclay told me on the bus that you didn't want them.

Moira continued, "But our dream was to make this movie, the product of our love."

"Speaking of the movie, you and Lairie had quite a catfight in the scene," I said.

"The child's unbalanced behavior suited her role in the film," Moira replied.

So the fight was real.

Next, Owen led in Lairie Naughton, who sat in her wet costume with pools of water surrounding the chair.

"We won't keep you long, lass," Frazier said.

Lairie looked as excited as an evangelical opening a gay conversion therapy center. "I'm happy to answer your questions, Chief Inspector."

"Did you see anything suspicious out there today?" I asked.

"No, I was too busy being an actress."

Frazier rubbed his chin. "You must be quite upset about what happened to your employer."

She laughed. "Upset? I thought Barclay Conall was a penny-pinching creep."

"But what happened to Barclay was tragic," Frazier said.

As if the guest star on a television mystery show, Lairie said, "The only tragedy was that his wife didn't join him. But if you want any information about Moira, you'll have to ask her brother-in-law Magnus."

Owen led in Magnus Conall, still in his tunic, kilt, and cloak.

Frazier said, "My condolences for the loss of your brother."

Magnus nodded and surveyed the room.

As the new lord of Conall Castle, is he planning on

redecorating? "Does your brother's will leave you Conall Castle?"

"Aye. I'm the middle brother."

"Will you make any changes in the hotel business?" I asked.

"Aye. I'll be the owner instead of Barclay."

"Magnus, did you see where your brother went after you finished acting in your scene?" Frazier asked.

The accountant shook his head and shafts of red surrounded his face like flames. "My brother liked to stroll around his property and play the laird of the land—rubbing it in my face, and in Fergus's too."

But did you rub out Barclay?

Next was youngest brother Fergus who aimed his long nose at Frazier. "I hope this won't take long. I'm famished."

And by the look of your shaking hands, in need of a drink. "Before his death, your brother wasn't too happy with you, was he?"

"My brother wasn't happy with anyone."

"Are you saying you believe Barclay jumped off that cliff?" Frazier inadvertently wrote on his hand instead of the pad.

Fergus looked up at the Medieval chandelier. "Only Barclay would know that, and he's gone."

"Do you have any idea what happened to your brother?" Frazier accidentally rubbed ink onto his thick thumb.

The restaurant manager scratched his thick hair. "Barclay wasn't happy lately. He and Moira weren't getting on, and there was some problem between him and Brody."

"About housekeeping?" Frazier asked.

The bags under Fergus's eyes bounced like pillows in a pillow fight. "You'll have to ask Brody."

Brody Naughton sat before us, tugging at his long beard.

Frazier asked, "Was there a problem between you and Barclay Conall?"

Brody's blue eyes turned to blue lines. "Barclay wasn't very...kind to his staff. He saw only the faults in others, including his family and friends."

Frazier leaned back in his chair. As it started to tumble backwards, I caught it. "Thank you, Professor." Getting his bearings, Frazier asked Brody, "What did you have against Barclay?"

"It's not a secret." Brody's strong jaw clenched. "My mother, Elsbeth Naughton, worked at the castle in Housekeeping. My dad, Robbie, was Caretaker."

Frazier smiled. "A big place like this requires a large staff. Most people who live at the tip in Conall work at the castle. My mother was bookkeeper until she passed a year ago."

Brody nodded. "I know. And like Kendric Conall, his son Barclay worked the staff extremely hard."

"Aye, I remember my mother keeping long hours in the office." Frazier rested an elbow on the arm of his chair, which slid off, causing his side to bang into the chair and his pen to fall out of his hand. Leaning down to retrieve it, he banged his head on the desk again. "Sorry."

"My folks were good people, like yours. And Barclay refused to bury them in the castle cemetery."

Frazier replied, "Since my dad was Chief Superintendent, both of my parents were buried in the inspector's lot."

Can we get back to the investigation?

Frazier added with a proud grin, "My dad taught me everything he knew." He turned over a page of his notepad and banged his wrist on the desk. "Sorry."

I wonder if his dad taught him coordination. "Brody, in the van on the way to the shoot, Barclay told me that you and he had a...personal relationship."

Frazier's wide jaw dropped. "You and Barclay got it

on, Brody? I mean, Mr. Naughton, you and the eldest Mr. Conall were intimate?"

Brody looked out the window. "It was a huge mistake." He glared me. "Something I'd like never to be reminded of again."

By killing Barclay?

The remaining interviews were uneventful, except for when Martin asked Frazier if Owen is in love with him. Frazier fell off the chair — literally — and then assured us his relationship with the young inspector was purely business. *At least on Frazier's part.*

After the inspectors left, Fergus seated us all in the Great Hall, where Hamish served lunch. Noah and I again shared our table with Taavi, Mom, Dad, Martin, and Ruben.

Dressed in another loud Hawaiian shirt and Bermuda shorts, Dad was first to dig into his pie. "Hey, Hamish, this is terrific. What's in it?"

Standing at our table, Hamish's button nose turned red. "Pieces of steak, carrots, mushroom, tomato paste, and spices."

Dad downed another huge piece, smacked his lips like a food critic, and said, "There's something else."

"Probably the ox kidney." Hamish left our table and whispered with Fergus at the buffet.

Dad moved on to his Scottish pudding, and the scent of cinnamon, fruit, and butter surrounded us.

Mom, looking like a lemon drop in a yellow top and culottes, pushed away her plate. "How can you eat at a time like this, Dad?"

"Yeah, I know it's a tragedy," Dad said, continuing to gobble down his dessert.

"It sure is!" Mom sighed. "A man was killed, and I didn't get a picture for Judy in Wisconsin!" Then she glared at Dad as if interrogating him under a spotlight. "Are there nuts in that pudding?"

"Nope," Dad replied, finishing his last mouthful.

Mom patted Noah's shoulder. "Then you can eat it, honey." She rummaged inside her lemon-yellow purse. "But just in case there are ground nuts in the crust, I brought your epinephrine."

I kissed Mom's cheek. "Thank you for taking care of Noah."

She chortled. "I've been watching out for Noah's nut allergy since he was a kid."

"But I always sensed Noah would grow up to *like* nuts." Dad burst out laughing.

Noah's handsome face turned the color of Mom's blouse. Desperate to change the subject, he asked, "How was your trip to the abbey, Mom?"

Mom replied, "It's exquisite. Tall, gothic, with gorgeous stained-glass windows. Judy can't understand why nuns don't live there anymore. I mean, there must still be women in Scotland who want to marry Jesus. In his pictures, Jesus was very handsome, like Noah with blond hair and blue eyes."

Not likely in Nazareth at the time.

"And Jesus could certainly rise to the occasion."

Mom hit Dad's shoulder playfully, and they shared a laugh.

Dad added, "But I'm guessing he'd be grumpy every Good Friday."

"Enough, Dad!" Mom held her stomach as she guffawed and then wiped her eyes with a napkin.

"Speaking of abbeys, *The Sound of Music* is on later this afternoon."

"How many times are you going to watch that movie, Dad?" Mom asked.

"The mountains are beautiful," Dad replied.

"There are mountains and an abbey here in northern Scotland!"

"It's not the same."

Mom slid to the edge of her seat. "There's one thing the Conall abbey has that was definitely not in *The Sound of Music*." She looked from side to side and then said, "When I was leaving, a leprechaun appeared at the doorway and wished me a 'nice bide.' That's Scottish talk for 'a nice stay.'"

Noah laughed. "You have the wrong country, Mom. Leprechauns hail from Ireland."

"Well, he must have taken a trip to Scotland, because there he was in the abbey," Mom said.

Intrigued, I asked, "Why do you think he's a leprechaun?"

Mom raised her iPhone. "See?"

A small, wiry, man of about ninety with long gray hair and a longer gray beard smirked at me. He wore a faded kelly-green work shirt and pants from another era.

Noah craned his neck to see the picture. "He's probably a poor local who finds shelter in the abbey when needed."

Mom stuck to her guns—or to her iPhone. "He had a mystical quality about him—as if he could read my thoughts."

"I'll take a walk over to the abbey sometime and see if he's there." My inner Sherlock Holmes appeared. "Maybe he knows something about Barclay Conall's murder."

Sipping his hot cocoa, Martin asked, "Speaking of which, what did you and the chief inspector uncover in your interviews, Nicky?"

I said between bites of my pudding, "Barclay was a tough boss like his father before him, which no longer matters since Magnus is the new owner of Conall Castle. Brody is angry with Barclay for not allowing him to bury his parents in the Conall Castle cemetery."

"Why should Barclay allow Brody to do that?" Ruben asked as he ate Martin's pudding.

"Brody's mother, Elsbeth, like Brody, worked here in

Housekeeping, and his father, Robbie, was Caretaker," I explained.

Dad stared straight ahead toward Magnus and Moira who were giggling with their heads together at the next table. He choked on his ale.

"What's wrong?" Mom patted his flabby back.

"Nothing." Dad wasn't a very good actor. "It just went down the wrong way."

Martin rested his cup on the large wooden table. "Nicky, are you holding out on us?"

Ruben explained, "Martin wants to know whose bags are being filled with whose pipes."

As if spoon-feeding chocolate cake to a dieter, I replied, "Brody and Barclay had a…moment, but Brody wants to forget it. Donal, the night waiter, seems interested in Brody, but Brody believes two men can't be in love."

"That's ridiculous!" everyone at the table said in unison like an acapella group.

Dad motioned over to Magnus and Moira. "Are brother number two and the grieving widow an item?"

I looked over as Magnus rested his hand on Moira's shoulder. "Sure seems like it to me." Then I glanced over at Fergus and Hamish arguing at the buffet. "And there seems to be trouble in fiancé paradise with brother number three and the day waiter."

"Are we shooting my scene today?" Taavi asked in actor mode.

"It's my scene too," Noah said, clearly ready to battle his son for star billing.

"Moira wants the shooting to continue," I said.

"Yeah! Costumes!" Taavi and Noah raced upstairs to change for the upcoming scenes.

I could barely keep a straight face (no pun intended) as I said to Martin, "Moira asked me if the film can be dedicated to Barclay."

"As long as I still get screenwriting credit." Martin sat

back in his chair. "You know, it's amazing how that headband hidden under Moira's wig takes a good ten years off her face. I wonder if *I* should try that."

"You'd need a hydraulic lift." Ruben kissed Martin's ear.

Martin asked, "Ruben, will you still love me when I'm old and decrepit?"

He replied, "Who knows? I can't go back in time."

I downed my usual supplements, plus the milk thistle, with Martin's hot cocoa. Then Martin (script in hand), Ruben (watch on wrist), and I headed over to the library. Thanks to the technicians, the camera, lights, and sound were already set for the upcoming scene. Noah, Taavi, Magnus, and Fergus arrived in their tunics, kilts, hose, sporran, brogues, and cloaks. Since Taavi and Noah looked like Scottish dolls, I couldn't help giving them each a big kiss on the cheek.

"Careful not to ruin the makeup!" My husband and son hurried to the makeup woman for a touch up.

Moira appeared in her blouse, vest, long shawl, skirt, and ghillies. The headband pulled her face tighter than a priest at the Communion wine. After I checked in with the DP, I asked Noah and Taavi to sit at the library desk for a rehearsal. Noah, a skilled actor, had clearly worked with Taavi on listening and reacting with emotional intensity. Though at first glance, the scene appeared to be about a tutor teaching the lord's son, the subtext was quite evident. The tutor, Noah (Oliver), was the only person at the castle who Taavi (Roddy) could trust.

When the lesson was over, Taavi rested an elbow on the desk. "I feel like a wee child who nobody ever notices."

"I notice ye," Noah said with a warm smile.

A tear filled Taavi's large dark eyes. "I know, Oliver." He stood and gazed out the window. "But with my father passed on, how will I ever be laird if nobody takes me seriously?"

Noah's paternal love for Taavi made the scene all the more touching. He stood next to Taavi. "Roddy, I have taught ye a great deal about numbers, words, history, Scotland, and even about God. Let me teach ye one more thing. 'It's a long road that doesn't have a turn in it.'"

Kind of like our "It gets better" slogan.

Taavi threw his arms around Noah's neck and they shared a hug.

When they released, Noah said, "Now tend to your studies, lad. I shall be back in a wee bit."

The rehearsal ended. The crew applauded and wiped the tears from their cheeks. Though the acting in the following two-shot was terrific, we had to reshoot, since Noah and Taavi kept leaning in closer to the camera, covering the other. After I threatened to tie them to their chairs, my two little Scottish hams behaved, and the scene went fine. Next, we did the close-ups. Each take was equally heart-wrenching.

Ruben breathed a sigh of relief as we moved on to rehearse the next scene. Magnus (Archibald) enters the library and lures Taavi (Roddy) into the hallway with a fake story that Oliver has asked to see him. With Ruben waving his watch like the revolutionary flag in *Les Miserables*, we ended the rehearsal and shot the short scene in one take.

The crew reset to shoot in the hallway. Noah coached the actors as Martin made sure they said every word exactly as written in his "masterpiece" screenplay. After I conferred with the DP, we rehearsed the scene. Finally, we were ready to shoot.

Taavi searched the hallway. "I don see Oliver."

"Follow me, laddie, and I'll take ye to him." Magnus led Taavi around the corner and down a hidden passageway. The crew followed—noisier than a rock concert ending with fireworks during a volcanic eruption.

"Cut!"

Once the crew quieted down, we continued the scene. Taavi exclaimed, "Where is he?"

"Your tutor isn't here, laddie. But your Uncle Archibald wants to talk to ye." Magnus grinned and rubbed his wide nose.

"I want Oliver!"

"Quiet now, laddie!" Magnus pulled on a brass wall sconce and the wall spun open—smack into Magnus's nose.

"Cut!"

An ice pack was applied. Upon removal, Magnus's already wide nose was doubled in size. We picked (no pun intended) up the scene at the reveal of the hidden room. Magnus pushed Taavi inside and then slid the wall closed as Taavi cried for Oliver.

Thankfully Taavi played in caves in Hawaii and doesn't have claustrophobia.

Fergus, as third brother Angus, appeared.

I whispered to Noah next to me, "Did Fergus just grow three inches?"

He whispered back, "He's wearing lifts in his shoes."

"Why are ye in the hidden wing, brother?" Fergus asked.

Magnus replied, "As laird of the castle, I can go wherever I like, brother."

"Ye won't be laird for long."

"How do ye know?"

Fergus drew his sword. "*This* told me."

Magnus took a sword off the wall. "*This* told me differently. And mine is longer."

"I don't think so."

"Maybe it's time we find out."

Magnus and Fergus spun around in duel position, dislodging their kilts, and we found out whose was longer.

"Cut!"

After our costumer repositioned their kilts, we redid

the long shot (pun intended).

Curtesy of Noah's fight choreography, the two brothers performed an aerobic swordfight down the hallway, leaping onto ledges, window seats, benches, and tables. When both men gasped for air like COPD victims with asthma after running a marathon and catching pneumonia, Magnus bent over in exhaustion. Taking advantage of the moment, Fergus said, "I always knew I would end on top, brother!" Then he waved his sword mightily and rammed it into Magnus bottom. Magnus fell to his knees, collapsed onto his back, shot his legs up into the air, screamed in release, and then his lifeless body crashed to the floor.

After Fergus adjusted his kilt (and no doubt scanned the hallway for oxygen), Moira (Fiona) rushed over to him, and they shared a long kiss. They were so into the scene, and each other, that his cloak and her shawl became entwined. They fell onto the floor shouting for help, rolling on top of each other again and again like a spool of yarn.

"Cut!"

The costumer untangled them and helped them to their feet. Then we repeated the long shot until we got it right. Given the complicated nature of the scene, the advanced hour, and Ruben's threat to use the sword and cut off my head (not the one you're thinking), I decided we didn't need to shoot close-ups for that scene. "Dinner break!"

A half hour later, I was back with my family and best friends for dinner at our table near the huge stone fireplace in the Great Hall. Donal served us leek and tattie soup (or leak and potato soup to us Yanks), seared Scottish salmon with parsnip puree and root vegetables, and mince pie. The small, handsome waiter asked, "How did the shooting go today?"

"We finished on time," Ruben said, eating his soup.

"My husband, the artist." Martin sipped his hot cocoa.

Taavi slapped hands with Noah. "Dad and I killed it."

"I like the billing." Noah smiled at our son.

I kissed Noah's cheek. "My swashbuckling husband choreographed quite a duel. Magnus and Fergus looked believable in battle."

Donal grimaced. "I'm not surprised."

Martin leaned over so far, he nearly landed in the mince pie. As if wishing at a well, he asked Donal, "Are the two remaining Conall brothers at odds?"

"My boss is at odds with everyone, especially the restaurant staff." Donal glanced over his shoulder at Fergus arguing with a busboy.

Dad motioned to Donal for a second piece of salmon. "It's not as good as meatloaf, but it hits the spot." He glanced at his watch. "I better eat fast. *Highlander* is on TV in a half hour."

Young Lairie appeared in front of us, wearing a white dress. "Are you all enjoying your dinners?"

Mom took a picture of Lairie and texted. Then she said, "Judy from Wisconsin thinks you look like a little angel."

Lairie giggled and pranced around the table. "Sometimes I pretend to be a ghost haunting the castle. Other times I imagine I'm a princess trapped here, or my favorite—the lady of the castle."

Eagerly connecting with another thespian, Taavi asked, "How come you didn't watch us shooting today?"

Lairie sighed like a has-been movie star. "I wanted to come, but my father made me strip all the beds and bring the sheets to the laundress." She leaned on the table and posed with the back of her hand over her forehead. "How I miss acting!"

Seems like you're doing a pretty good job of it right now.

Taavi milked it more than a goat farmer. "I had two scenes with my Dad, and then Magnus pushed me into the hidden room that you showed me!"

"There's nothing in there but an old bed and bookcase.

Weren't you bored?" Lairie asked.

"Fergus and Magnus were sword-fighting outside," Taavi explained.

"I can't believe I missed that!" Lairie wringed her hands. "Ugh! I feel like Cinderella unable to go to the ball!"

"If you need a fairy godmother, call Martin." Ruben moved on to the vegetable puree.

"Or call my husband, if you'd like a wicked stepmother," Martin retorted.

"I've already got one of those." A line appeared across the young girl's forehead. "My mother was a waitress here. She ran off with the bartender when I was a baby and never came back. So now I work for the vicious Conall family who treat me worse than a scullery maid!"

Tears filled Mom's eyes. "How horrible! You poor little thing."

Lairie seemed to be auditioning for Scarlett O'Hara. "I've learned to live without a mother, keep my head up high, and forge through the storm of life."

Taavi poked my ribs. "Isn't she terrific? Lairie's even more dramatic than you and Dad."

They say men marry their fathers.

"Lairie!" Brody Naughton towered over his daughter. "I thought you were going to do turn-down service."

Always the font of compassion and diplomacy, Noah said, "We were enjoying our visit with Lairie."

"She shouldn't be *visiting*. She should be *working*," Brody said with a sneer.

My sweet Noah rose to his feet. "I don't think there is any harm in the girl making friends with us."

"And why would a rich American man want to befriend my young daughter?"

Donal arrived at Brody's side. "Let them eat in peace, Brody."

The bearded man stared him down. "And what do *you* have to do with this?"

Noah clenched his fists. "You don't have to shout at Donal."

"I'll shout at whomever I like!" Brody replied.

Noah looked unhappier than a conservative politician at an alternative energy rally. I had never seen him get angry at anyone—other than me when I yank the bedcovers in winter.

Dad glanced up at Noah. "Sit down, boy. There's no need to make a scene."

Not exactly a motto Noah, Taavi, and I live by.

Surprised at his father's order, Noah slowly sat down.

"Excuse us. We need to get to work." Brody left with his arm around Lairie. "You shouldn't speak out against your employers."

"The Conalls are arrogant Cretans who treat us like the hired help," Lairie said.

"That's because we *are* the hired help."

After they were gone, Donal said, "I apologize."

"Why?" Noah added, "*You* weren't the rude one, Donal."

"Brody's bark is worse than his bite," Donal said.

"And you're such a sweet young man, Donal." Mom pointed to Dad. "I understand first-hand about seeing the soft spot in a bear." Then she looked at Noah and me adoringly. "And I know we love who we love." She squeezed Donal's hand. "So don't give up on Brody."

Donal squeezed back, blinked back tears, and hurried off to the buffet.

I turned to Noah. "Are you all right?"

He nodded. "I don't know what Donal sees in Brody. There's no excuse for that kind of rudeness."

Mom pointed to her iPhone. "That's exactly what Judy just said."

At the next table, Moira shouted, "When are you going to do it, Magnus?"

Her brother-in-law smirked. "Maybe the brownies will

do it for me."

When their voices returned to whispers, Martin asked me, "What do you think the new lord and old lady of the castle are arguing about?"

"Magnus not doing the audit is my guess," Ruben said, eating Martin's mince pie.

"What's a brownie?" Taavi asked.

Dad must have recalled the Scottish folklore he learned on his trip to Scotland as a young man. "A brownie is a good-natured elf." He pointed to Martin. "They look like Martin, if he was green."

Noah and I froze. An invisible Scottish lightbulb appeared over our heads.

Sensing our cognitions, Martin placed his napkin onto the table and looked off into the distance dramatically. "I hear the stage calling me."

"Brownies usually travel in pairs." Dad winked at Ruben.

"I'm ready for my close-up," Ruben said without hesitation.

"Judy wants to know what everyone is talking about," Mom said.

Martin explained, "The Chief Inspector and his young lovelorn assistant inspector are as incompetent as a politician doing a government ethics probe."

"And as annoying as a proctologist with a neurological disorder and long fingernails," Ruben added.

I slid to the edge of my seat. "So, it is up to the Sherlock Holmes and John Watson of Conall Castle to delve into the den of drama (*try saying that three times fast*) and investigate the case." I winked at Martin and Ruben. "With a little help from our friends."

Noah grinned maniacally. "Good thing I packed my makeup case."

Later that evening, Noah and I peeked out from behind a stone wall. The silver stars in the cobalt sky were our only company.

On cue two brownies arrived in front of the castle room. That's castle-ese for the lord's bedroom. Courtesy of Noah's makeup skills, Martin and Ruben sported green faces and hands. Thanks to our film's costumer, our friends wore green shorts, stockings, high-backed shoes with tassels, tunics, and pointy caps. My touch as director led my department head and his husband to walk on their knees—with their shoes attached to them.

Ruben said, "I feel like a character in the *Wizard of Oz*."

"Toto?" Martin asked.

Ruben glared at his spouse. "No."

"The Wicked Witch of the West?"

"No."

"Miss Gulch? An evil monkey?"

"A Munchkin of course!" Ruben shouted.

Focus guys!

Magnus came to the turret window in his boxer shorts and did a doubletake. When Martin and Ruben, or rather the brownies, motioned to him, Magnus climbed out through the window and followed them to a grassy knoll nearby. Clearly having had one Scotch too many (no pun intended), Magnus squinted his green eyes at the green elves. "Are you wee guys real?"

Martin and Ruben giggled together, holding hands. They tried to jump up and down but toppled over.

I whispered in Noah's ear, "Hopefully they won't need knee replacements."

After taking a swig from his glass, Magnus rubbed his wide nose. "What do you brownies want with me?"

They were back on their knees (no pun intended). I was surprised when Martin's high-pitched voice didn't crack Magnus's glass. His accent was a cross between Scottish, Yiddish, and Hungarian. "We came from the world underneath the grass, tree roots, and sheep poop."

Sheep poop?

Ruben sounded like a train whistle blown under a helicopter during a tornado. His Scottish had a Translyvanian flair. "We are here to welcome the new laird of Conall Castle. And to lead you to the pot of gold."

Noah whispered in my ear, "Isn't that only for leprechauns in Ireland?"

Surprisingly, greedy Magnus bought it. "Where is it?"

"Not so fast." Martin waved a tiny finger at him. "We need to know if you are worthy."

"And if you aren't, you'll come up short-handed, like him." Ruben laughed at Martin.

Can the comedy guys!

Magnus ran a hand through his red hair and his bicep bulged out of his T-shirt. "How will you know if I'm worthy?"

"If we find you to be honest with us," Martin said.

"And if I'm not?"

"You will join your brother," Ruben said.

"Fergus?" Magnus laughed. "He's in town."

"Not *that* brother." Martin pointed toward the countryside.

"The one who fell off the cliff into the ocean," Ruben explained.

Magnus's face drained of color. "It was you brownies who did that?"

"I won't say we did, and I won't say we didn't." Martin winked at him. "But I will say he hit the sea like a toxic oil spill."

Get to the questions!

Magnus took another sip of his drink. "What is it you want to know?"

Martin got right to the point (pun intended). "Who have you been lying with in the heather?"

Magnus replied, "You're a bunch of nosey brownies, aren't you?"

"Me, nosey?" Martin somehow asked with a straight

(no pun intended) face.

Ruben said to Magnus, "If you'd like that pot of gold, I'd answer, lad."

"Magnus took another sip of his drink, swayed a bit, and then sat on a tree stump. "My woman is named Moira."

I knew it!

"She's the wife of my dead brother."

Martin sat at Magnus's feet. "And you and Moira had been together before Barclay's death?"

Magnus nodded, and his red hair dropped over his forehead.

"How scandalous!"

Said the men in green stockings with tassels on their shoes.

"She's a desk clerk at the hotel." A tear rimmed his eye. "I love her."

Martin and Ruben smiled at each other, no doubt remembering their multitude of years together and their two grown daughters.

The producer in Ruben took over quickly. "Did you and Moira skim the hotel books?"

"Why do you need to know that?" Magnus asked.

"Why do you need our pot of gold?" Ruben sat at Magnus's other foot.

"What if we did?" He groaned. "My dad, Kendric, was a tough boss, like my brother, Barclay, after him. Penny-pinchers! That's what they were."

Martin said, "How convenient that you are the accountant."

Magnus stared up at the sky as if watching his life in scenes of star constellations. "There was nothing convenient about it...with my brother watching every move Moira and I made in the office."

"So when your brother caught on to your stealing, you threw Barclay off that cliff, and took his wife as your own," Martin said, as if reading the happily ever after ending of a children's story.

"Right. No! I didn't kill my brother," Magnus said.

"Did Moira?" Ruben asked.

"Moira wouldn't kill anyone," Magnus replied.

Neither would Lady Macbeth.

Magnus stood on shaky legs. "You two brownies are putting words in my mouth." After a gulp of his drink, he asked, "Now I told you what you want to know. Where's my treasure?"

Martin and Ruben giggled. "You'll have to catch us first."

Even with him drunk, my money's on Magnus.

Martin and Ruben hurried on their arthritic knees toward a side entrance into the castle. Magnus followed them, swaying like a flag in a hurricane. When they had disappeared, Noah and I headed inside after them.

After my eyes adjusted to the light, I followed the younger (grrr) Noah down a long hallway and then into another passageway. Suddenly, a hand grabbed my arm, and I fell backwards. I soon realized I was lying on a bed with Noah on top of me (not all together a bad thing). A lamp illuminated the small room, and I looked up at Martin and Ruben sitting on either side of the bed.

"Where are we?" I asked as I (unfortunately) slid out from underneath Noah.

"In the hidden room," Ruben whispered.

"Don't you remember from the shoot today?" Martin mimed Magnus pulling on the wall sconce and pushing Taavi into the secret room.

"Why are we in here?" I whispered.

Martin placed a green hand on his green hip. "Did you hit your head, Nicky?"

Noah explained to me, "I think we're all hiding from Magnus."

We heard an odd noise, like a butcher slicing meat. And then a loud thud. Martin slowly peeled open the walled doorway, and the four of us snuck a peek.

Noah said, "Nicky, look!"

I followed Noah's gaze to Magnus, laying on the stone floor with the very bloody knight's sword lodged into his stomach. *The sword in the stone.*

CHAPTER FOUR

The next morning, I was back in the Great Hall at my family's table for breakfast. Hamish MacAlastair placed hot tea, oatcakes, and fruit in front of us. I readied my stack of supplements, including the milk thistle capsules.

I didn't get much sleep the night before, thinking about finding Conall brother number two with a sword in his stomach. My mind was swirling from Chief Inspector Lennox Frazier's (and my) subsequent interrogation of everyone at the castle. Upon leaving, Frazier had knocked over so many artifacts in the castle hallway, Inspector Owen Steward had to bend over backwards (pun intended) rescuing them.

Hamish towered over our table. "Do you folks have everything you need?"

"Can I get some hot cocoa?" Martin asked, wearing a mauve bowtie and sweater vest. "Without cocoa, I feel dried out and decrepit."

"As you can tell by looking at him," Ruben added in a mauve leisure suit.

Martin glared at his husband. Then they both burst out laughing and shared a kiss.

The waiter smiled. "I hope Fergus and I last as long as you two."

Especially now that Fergus is laird of Conall Castle. "I'm sure that you, Fergus, and the entire hotel staff are still reeling from what happened last night."

It took Hamish a moment to realize what I was talking

about. "Aye, of course. Fergus is beside himself over losing both of his brothers so tragically."

Noah nudged my arm, and I glanced over at Fergus in his restaurant manager suit whispering conspiratorially with Moira. In her cherry, low-cut dress, Moira left Fergus at the buffet and sat at a table by herself on the other side of the enormous stone fireplace. Seizing the opportunity, I excused myself and approached her. "Moira, what a shock about Magnus. And so soon after losing Barclay. You must be devastated."

She craned her neck toward me as if I were a fly on her nose. "Aye."

"Would you like to join my family, friends, and me for breakfast? In difficult times, being with other people can help."

"No, thank you. I need to compose myself for our shoot after breakfast."

I did a doubletake. "You'd like to continue the movie?"

She nodded stoically. "I consulted my local psychic. She confirmed that it's what Barclay and Magnus want." Clearly summoning up the skills she had learned as an actress, Moira lifted her sagging jowls and said like the heroine in a gothic romance novel, "I will do everything in my power to grant their wish."

And to star in their movie. "Of course."

When I returned to my table, Hamish was saying, "Fergus and I haven't fully processed losing his brothers." His jaw tightened. "He got back to the castle late last night. I was already asleep."

Martin said, "If everyone in the castle was murdered after nine p.m., Ruben would still sleep like a coma victim."

"Only if *you* were murdered, dear." Ruben held up the fruit bowl. "Fruit?"

"No, thank you. I already have one, and it's overripe, decayed, and way past it's prime." Martin dug into his oatcakes.

Hamish crinkled his button nose. "Is there anything else I can get anyone?"

Martin cleared his throat. "My hot cocoa?"

"Right!" Hamish disappeared.

With only family and friends in ear shot, Dad swallowed an oatcake whole and then said, "Two Conalls down. Definitely seems like a mass murderer is on the loose in this hotel."

Mom fixed the collar of Dad's Hawaiian shirt and said as if asking me to take out the garbage, "You should find the murderer soon, Nicky."

"I'm working with Frazier and Owen," I said.

Dad did a spit-take with his tea. "Those two guys are as useless as the media when Russia hacks into an election."

Mom glanced at her iPhone. "Judy says it's up to you to solve the case, Nicky. Or should I say, 'Sherlock Holmes.' And to my adorable baby boy, 'Watson.'" She kissed Noah's cheek, leaving a mark of two cranberry lips.

Noah's face turned the color of Mom's cranberry dress.

"How did the role-play go last night, Martin?" Dad asked as if he were Martin and Ruben's manager.

"I was wonderful!" Martin said. "Despite playing opposite an amateur."

Ruben guffawed. "May I remind you that was the *fifth* role-play I performed for Nicky and Noah."

"Mine too! And may I remind *you* that pales on a resume next to *my* Broadway credits." Martin sniffed proudly.

"Did they have paper back then?" Ruben asked.

Taavi asked at the edge of his seat, "When do I get to do a role-play, Pop?"

"You don't. You're too young," I replied.

Like a conservative politician speaking about a five-year-old with an assault weapon, Noah said, "Taavi has to learn some time."

"I'll think about it," I replied.

Dad asked, "What did you guys learn about Magnus — before he kicked the castle bucket?"

Noah explained, "Our hunch was right. Magnus was skimming the Conall Castle books, and Barclay found out about it."

Martin waved Noah away like a tax auditor at a megachurch. "More importantly, Magnus was cuckolding his brother Barclay by carrying on at the castle with cagey Moira!" *Try saying that three times fast.*

"If you need an actress for a role-play, I'm available." Mom patted the side of her blonde-tipped hair. "As you know from our Alaska cruise, I have the experience."

"And don't forget your Dad. My role-play in Alaska was award-worthy." He reached under his shirt and pulled out his half four-leaf clover necklace. "And in my younger days, I spent some time in Scotland."

"I'll keep that in mind." I asked Mom and Dad, "What's on the agenda for you two today?"

Mom replied, "Judy did some research online and said Dad and I should take the train to do some sightseeing." She glanced at her iPhone. "There are some beautiful locations like Skara Brae, the Loch an Eilein, Chanonry Ness, the Quiraing Walk, Loch Lomand, and Callanish Stones."

"I'm busy." Dad finished his tea. "*Brigadoon* is on TV."

Undaunted, Mom flipped through photos on her iPhone. "There's also the Falls of Foyers and Plodda Falls."

"Not happening." Dad said, "*Niagara Falls* comes on next."

"And I want to see The Great Moor of Rannoch."

"No can do." Dad stuffed a banana into his mouth. "*Wuthering Heights* follows.

Mom sighed. "Well I'm not missing Dunrobin Castle, Urquhart Castle, Cawdor Castle, Dunnottar Castle, and Blair Castle!"

"I am. They're showing *The Last Castle* before the news."

"You are the most impossible man to travel with, Dad!" Mom rose in anger.

"No he isn't." Ruben pointed to Martin. "Meet the man who packed enough diapers to transport a daycare center across the globe."

Martin slammed his fist on the table. "At least I didn't pack a dildo in the shape of an alien from outer space!"

"That was a low blow, Martin!"

"Obviously!"

As Martin and Ruben argued, and Mom and Dad bickered, Taavi cried, "I want to do a role-play and help you and Dad solve the case, Pop!"

Noah let out a piercing whistle and everyone froze. After he pointed to me, I said like a teacher calling an end to recess, "Mom, we are at the northernmost tip of Scotland. The places you mentioned are hours away in various directions. There's no way you can see all of them by train. Go to the front desk and ask for information about the available day tours. You'll be safe sightseeing on those. Dad, retire to your room and watch as much television as you like. Martin, Ruben, Noah, and Taavi, come with me. We have a film to shoot." *Before we all shoot each other.*

Taavi and Noah slapped hands. "You're playing our song!"

Noah, Taavi, and I headed to the main hallway, where we found Lairie and Brody in jeans and sweatshirts standing near the grand staircase.

"Please, Dad!" Lairie clutched at the wooden sculpture of a lion on the bannister as if it were her Academy Award. "There is a lion in my heart, begging to be let out of its cage. If I don't act, I'll expire!"

"You aren't a warranty, Lairie," said Brody.

"No, I'm an actress!"

"You're a girl working as a maid when you aren't in

school. We aren't Conall royalty. We're the hired help. And I don't want you to lose your job."

"The Conalls are monstrous bosses and horrible people." Lairie clenched her fists and her eyes doubled in size. "Look how horribly Barclay treated you when you tried to be his friend, Dad. And they wouldn't even let you bury my grandparents in their precious cemetery!"

"Lower your voice, Lairie," her father said.

She cried, "I don't care if the Conalls hear me! And I don't care if I lose my job!"

"Well, *I* care." Brody stared down at his daughter.

Taavi smiled at the fourteen-year-old girl. "I'm acting in the next scene, Lairie."

Noah cleared his throat.

Taavi gave Noah the hang loose sign. "With my Dad as supporting actor."

After holding back a chuckle, I said to Brody, "It's fine with me if Lairie watches."

Brody tugged at his red beard. "It's fine with you, is it? Since you aren't Lairie's father, we'll file that under 'nobody cares.'"

Noah came between us. "You may be able to bully Lairie and Donal, but you won't talk that way to my husband, or to me."

Was that my kind and sweet Noah?

Brody glared at Noah. "If you weren't a guest at this hotel, I'd take you outside and do more than talk to you."

"I'm ready when you are."

Scott appeared at the top of the staircase. "Noah, can you come up here a minute?"

Dad must be having trouble with the remote control.

I nodded at Noah. He brushed past Brody and hurried up the stairs. Resting a hand on Taavi's shoulder, I said, "Excuse us. We have a movie to make." Then I led my son down the corridor to the secret passageway. The crew had already set up the lights, camera, and sound equipment.

The costumer stole away Taavi, while I discussed the logistics of the scene with the DP.

Ruben and Martin sat on a leather bench nearby. As usual, Ruben was glued to his watch, and Martin was riveted by his script. When Noah and Taavi arrived in costume, we rehearsed the scene. Noah (as Oliver, the tutor) walks down the hallway searching for Taavi (as young Roddy Conall). When Noah hears moaning from behind the wall, he bangs on it. When the wall bangs back, Noah presses on the wall, the molding, and finally the sconce. The wall opens to a shot of Taavi in the hidden room, sitting on the bed in tears. Noah sits next to him, and he and Taavi embrace. After Noah wipes away Taavi's tears, they strategize their revenge on Fergus (Uncle Angus) and Moira ("Mommy Dearest" Fiona).

The scene ended with Noah saying, "I believe it is time for us to teach ye uncle and mither a wee lesson, lad."

Taavi's eyes gleamed like spotlights. "I will enjoy learning *that* lesson, tutor."

The rehearsal ended, and Noah gave Taavi some acting notes (like, "If you cover my face with yours, I'm taking you out of our will."). Next, we slated and filmed the two-shot, and then each close-up.

When I was satisfied that we had what I needed, I called for lunch. Noah and Taavi left to change back into their clothes. I accidentally overheard two men arguing around the corner (with my ear pressed against the wall). So, I hid beside the grandfather clock nearby and watched.

"Nothing will change with Fergus as owner of the castle." Brody held a box full of cleaning fluids and rested his foot on the first step of the back staircase.

Cute little Donal Blair stood beside him in a baby blue T-shirt and jeans. "I work for Fergus in the restaurant, remember? He treats the staff like slaves. That is, except for Hamish." Making the quote sign with his small fingers, he added, "His fiancé."

Brody rested the box on a long black leather bench. "Magnus took everything Barclay had, including Barclay's wife. He knew the managers were onto him. So he had no use for us. Magnus was a horrible owner, and we had no use for him."

"Was he worse than Barclay?"

"No." Brody's face hardened. "Barclay was a tyrant. Nothing any of us managers did was ever right."

"I'm sure something you did for Barclay was right." Donal seemed to regret saying it.

"How long are you going to throw that rotten tomato at me?"

Donal rammed his hands inside his pants pockets. "I just don't understand what you saw in Barclay."

"That makes two of us."

The sweet Donal was back. "Brody, I knew I was gay since I was a lad. So, I'm confused about you and Barclay."

"I told you it was a mistake."

"I mean, you and Barclay were married to women."

"I remember, Donal."

"And I know it's none of my business—"

"That's right. It isn't." Brody reached for the box.

Donal blocked his way. "But how did you and Barclay…do what you did?"

"It isn't important."

"It's important to me."

"Why?"

"You know why."

Brody stroked his beard and sighed. "Barclay and I were like two mangy dogs in heat."

How romantic.

"He hated me afterward. And I hated him, and myself too."

Donal asked, "Because you two were in love?"

Brody laughed. "It might have been lust. But it definitely wasn't love. Two men can't be in love."

Donal said what I was thinking, "So you can have sex with a man but not be in love with one? Don't you think you're cutting yourself short?"

Or prompting someone else to do it?

Brody ran a thick hand through his blond locks. "Why do you do this, Donal?"

"Do what?"

"Try to get inside my mind."

I think Donal wants to get inside something more than your mind.

Donal said, "I thought we were friends, Brody."

"We are."

"Can't friends talk about their feelings?"

"Not *men* friends."

"Then let's break the mold."

Brody laughed bitterly. "Aren't you the wee psychiatrist, Donal?"

"Brody, I'm not trying to psychoanalyze you. I'm asking these questions because I care."

"Don't care."

"I can't help it."

"Yes, you can."

Donal gasped. "How can you be so cruel?"

Their blue eyes met. Suddenly, Brody threw his arms around Donal, drew him in close, and kissed him forcefully on the lips. After Donal came up for air, he kissed Brody back, massaging the rippling muscles on the bigger man's mountainous shoulders and wide back. Brody cupped Donal's bubble butt and squeezed. They kissed again, more passionately.

I should have filmed that instead of Martin's movie.

Then Brody released him. "This can't happen, Donal."

"Why, because you want to continue living in the shadows, hiding from your real feelings?"

Brody's face filled with rage. "I don't have feelings for you."

"That's not what your body just told me. You're

hearing your father's voice in your head, saying you aren't a real man because you love another man. But your father died with your mother in that plane crash. His homophobic thoughts should have died with him."

Brody pushed Donal away. "You don't know what you're talking about!"

Donal landed on the bench with tear-stained eyes. "I know what I feel. And the ghost of your dad can't change that."

Brody clenched his fists. "Don't speak about my parents."

The tears slid down Donal's cheeks. "Brody, I'll never understand why you hate me."

Brody rested his head in his hands. "I don't hate you."

"Then why can't we—"

"I told you! I can only do that with someone I don't like."

"And what does that say about you, Brody?"

"It says there's no future for you and me. So get off my back, Donal."

Donal groaned as if hit in the stomach. "All of your horrible words won't change what I feel for you. And what I think you feel for me."

"I don't want to hurt you, Donal."

"Then stop hurting me!"

Brody rubbed his forehead. "I want to love you, like you want."

"Then do it! Please, Brody, love me." Donal stood and walked toward him with outstretched arms.

"I can't." Brody hurried up the steps.

As Donal wept like the star of a daytime drama, I slipped away. Trying to find my path back to the main staircase, I must have taken one turn too many. As I reached an unfamiliar hallway, I heard a loud crash. Walking backwards, I tripped over something in my path. Scrambling to my feet, I realized it was Inspector Owen

Steward, on all fours next to me. *It's not what you're thinking.*

"I beg your pardon, Professor." Owen rose with a brass lantern in his hand. "Lennox, that is, the Chief Inspector and I were searching the castle for clues about the murders, when he knocked into this." His large Adam's Apple bobbed up and down like a rubber ball on a trampoline. He put the lantern back on its shelf. "Of course, anyone could have knocked over the lantern since it was sticking out of the wall. And we, that is Lennox, that is the Chief Inspector and I, aren't exactly sure that they were in fact murders."

I couldn't resist. "So you and Lennox, that is the Chief Inspector, think Magnus Conall stabbed *himself* with the knight's sword?"

"Hello, Professor." Frazier came out from behind the heavy brocade burgundy curtains at the nearby turret. The bottom edge of the curtain was lodged inside his shoe, so he plummeted to the floor.

Owen immediately assisted Frazier to his feet. "Are you all right there, Lennox, I mean Chief Inspector?"

"I believe so." He stumbled into the wall, knocking over the lantern again.

Rail-thin Owen seemed to enjoy holding the stocky Frazier in his arms a tad too long. "If you feel faint or unwell, you can rest on the window seat, Lennox, I mean, sir."

"I'm fine, Owen, agh Inspector." Frazier dusted himself off and walked toward me. "What are you doing in this wing of the castle, Professor?"

I assume that's castle-talk for 'this neck of the woods.' "To be honest, I'm lost."

Frazier replied, "Understandable. I'd be lost too if I hadn't played here from time to time as a lad. It's a big place." He spread his arms and knocked over a vase.

Owen caught it in mid-air and placed it back on the fireplace mantel. "No harm done, Lennox, I mean, sir." He scooped up the lantern and replaced it on the shelf.

"Have you found any clues, Professor?" Frazier asked.

Since Frazier was headed for an expensive-looking statue, I led him to sit next to me on the window seat. "Please, call me Nicky."

"All right, Nicky. What has the famous college theatre professor and amateur sleuth uncovered?"

I filled him in on what I knew. Since Frazier couldn't find his notepad and pen, Owen took notes.

Owen read them back to us like a court transcript. "Barclay was a tyrant as a boss. Magnus stole from the hotel intake. Fergus mistreats the restaurant staff except for Hamish, his fiancé. Fergus disappears at night, which angers Hamish. Moira had a thing with Magnus. Barclay had a thing with Brody. Donal has a thing for Brody."

It suddenly occurred to me. "I wonder."

"What is it?" Frazier slid to the edge of his seat.

I stopped him from falling into my lap. "The Conall brothers' parents died in a car accident off a cliff a year ago. I wonder if that has anything to do with somebody bumping off Barclay and Magnus Conall?"

"I doubt that." Frazier scratched at his shaggy-dog brown hair. "Brody's folks died in a plane crash recently. My dad passed from a heart attack, and my mom from cancer. It's tragic, but older people do leave us."

Owen stood before us proudly. "Lennox's, I mean the Chief Inspector's father was Chief Superintendent."

"I remember."

"As do I, Nicky. Dad taught me everything I know." Frazier stood and stepped on my toe. After I screamed, he said, "Sorry. My fault."

Owen said, "But it could happen to anyone, Lennox, I mean, sir."

As they led me back to the main hallway, I ducked, leaned away, and cringed as Frazier knocked over artifacts, pictures, a maid, and a window washer. Like a circus juggler, Owen caught each one, avoiding disaster.

At the main staircase, I asked, "How is *your* investigation coming along, Frazier?"

"Just fine," Owen replied. "The Chief Inspector is a mastermind investigator." He smiled proudly. "I'll bet you thought I was going to call the Chief Inspector 'Lennox,' as I do at the police service station. But I remembered this time to address Lennox as 'Chief Inspector.'" He whispered, "Since we are on a case."

"What exactly have you found out?" I asked.

Frazier replied, "There were no prints or fibers on either of the dead bodies, or on the knight's sword. We spoke with everyone at the castle, and nobody saw or heard anything. Everyone had the opportunity to kill both Barclay and Magnus."

"So you have nothing," I said.

"Not true, Professor." Owen waved his notepad. "Based on what you've told us, we now have a motive for each suspect." He nodded toward Frazier in awe and respect. "I believe the Chief Inspector is off to a very strong start."

After Frazier and Owen left, I took advantage of my break from filming. Weaving through the castle corridors like an intoxicated mouse in a maze, I stopped at a large bar to pilfer a bottle of whiskey. Then I continued past the armor in the front hallway and opened the heavy wooden door to daylight.

Walking along the bridge and then on the cobblestone walkway, the sun bathed my face in warmth, and the emerald green grass waved to me in the soft early summer breeze. In minutes, the sprawling decayed stone of the old abbey appeared stoically. As the structure grew larger, I marveled at the Conall crest on the white stone molding and the beautiful stained-glass windows.

Arriving at the front of the abbey, I made my way up the white stone steps, and pulled on the large bronze latch fastened to the wide birch door, just escaping a hernia.

Upon reaching the entryway of the historic structure, the colored shafts of sunlight, cool air, musty odor, and aura of ancient secrets permeated my senses. I walked into the worship area and stood beside a stone column opposite the altar. Tired from my walk, I sat on a nearby stone bench, imagining nuns holding their services at that very spot hundreds of years ago.

"All bauchle, are ye? Rest a tad."

I glanced over at the doorway to the next room. A short, thin, wiry man of about ninety years old with long gray hair and a long gray beard was before me. *Mom's leprechaun.* As in Mom's picture, he wore frayed, worn-out kelly-green work clothes. I rose. "I'm staying at Conall Castle to direct a movie." Offering my hand, I said, "Nicky Abbondanza."

"I know who ye be." As if Merlin the magician, he waved his hands in the air. "Ah know everythin'."

I got closer to him. "Do you live here in the abbey?"

He nodded. "Fer goin' on seventy year. Me faither were caretaker afore me."

I saw the light. Literally. A shaft of golden light from a stained-glass window blinded me, so I stepped to the old man's other side. "You were caretaker of the abbey?"

"I were."

"And you still live here?"

He shrugged his narrow shoulders. "Ware else would ye expect me to live?"

Sitting on a stone bench nearby, I said, "You must have seen quite a lot over the years."

He snickered. "Aye. But I don clype. Not a word have I ever said."

And deer don't shed ticks.

I held up the whiskey bottle. "I don't drink with a man whose name I don't know."

The man sat on the bench faster than the relative of a rich man at a funeral. "Ewan Baird." He held out a brown-spotted, veiny, bone-thin hand.

I passed him the bottle. Ewan unscrewed the top and took a long swig. Then he handed me back the whiskey.

Glancing at his yellowed saliva dribbling down the bottle, I said, "Enjoy, Ewan."

After taking another long drink, he replied, "Ye a good frein." He quickly finished a quarter of the bottle. "Now don thin I are a drunk. I jes like me whiskey from time to time. Same as any Jimmy."

I gazed around the room. "This is some place. I imagine a time when the Conalls frequented the abbey to pray."

He laughed uproariously, revealing blackened teeth. "They came to footer about mostly."

I smiled. "And you saw it all?"

"Aye." He took another swig.

Where's nosey Martin when I need him? "You must remember the owners before Barclay."

"Aye. Kendric and Emilia."

"I heard they died in a car accident off the cliff a year ago."

"That's the blether."

"You don't believe it?"

"I believe a body were happy about it."

My Sherlock Holmes persona emerged. "You think someone killed them, put them in that car, and pushed it over the cliff?"

"I do."

"Who?"

When he hesitated, I started to take the bottle back. He grabbed it and took another long drink. "A wain of theirs, I gather."

"Which child?"

"Any of them, I suspect."

"In order to inherit the castle and grounds?"

"Wouldn't you wan it?"

I nodded. "It's a beautiful place."

After another swig, he said, "That's why I corrie in here, so nobody will find me. A body who knows secrets may meet Black Donald fast."

"You think the Conall sons have secrets?"

"Not only the wains. The mither and faither too."

I slid closer to him. "Emilia and Kendric had secrets, did they?"

"From each other mostly. Kendric were in his office all the time, always stewin' about somethin'. Barclay were like his faither. Workin' all the time. Magnus were like his mither. Spendin' the money. Emilia liked comin' to the abbey."

"And Moira was caught between them all?"

After another long drink, he said, "That lassie has always been trouble. Split those two brothers apart like a boulder in a loch."

"Which brother loved her more?"

"Neither."

I did a doubletake. "I know Barclay and Moira had a troubled marriage. But I thought Moira and Magnus were in love."

"They were." He raised his hand as if on the witness stand. "But Magnus's first love were Fenella. She were a waitress at the castle some fifteen year ago." He sighed. "A beauty of a lassie. Long blonde hair like gold, and eyes blue as the sea." Elbowing me in the side, he added, "And her tiny titties pointed up like a cliff. You a tittie man, Nicky?"

"I prefer pectoral muscles, Owen."

"Aye. Queer then are ye?"

"As queer as trying to milk a bull."

"Ye come here with that blond lad and the wee laddie."

"They are my husband and son."

"Aye. Times has changed."

"But people haven't changed so much." Getting back to my investigation, I said, "I've known women like

Fenella."

"Aye. She could swear better than any Jimmy in Scotland. And beat him at arm-wrestlin' too." He smiled. "But fifteen year ago, Magnus and Fenella were in love. Real love. I seen them here at the abbey many a night."

Fishing without a pole (no pun intended), I asked, "Why didn't Magnus marry Fenella?"

"He wanted to. But Kendric said it were beneath his lad to merrit a waitress. So Fenella were merrit to Brody Naughton who worked in Housekeeping with his mither, Elsbeth."

"And Brody's marriage to Fenella failed?" I asked like a gossip columnist at the Oscars' red carpet.

"Aye. Brody were and is a goo goblin."

"A what?"

"He were like you. A Captain Cock. A rump divider. A ball juggler."

Who knew the Scottish had so many names for being gay?

"Brody favored Barclay, and Barclay were interested in Brody...but only for a wee time."

"But why did Brody marry Fenella?"

"Brody's fither, Robbie, the caretaker of the castle, pushed the lad. 'Be a man' and all that blether. Kendric did the same to Barclay, pushing him to merit Moira. The truth be, a body be what a body be."

"I agree with you there, Ewan."

He winked at me. "I thought ye would." After another sip, he added, "It were not a surprise that Barclay and Moira never had a wain. Brody must have done the deed once with Fenella though, since Lairie came along. But right after dropping the little lassie, Fenella seen she weren't cut out to be a mither. So she run off with the bartender, a huge lad called Balfour." He giggled. "I thin you'd a liked the look of that strappin' lad."

Coming to the point (no pun intended), I asked, "Who do you think killed Barclay and Magnus, and Kendric and

Emilia before them?"

Owen scratched as his long beard. "I knew them boys since they were wee lads. I warned them to be caw canny. Ye ne'er know what evil lurks. But they did naw listen. I warned their mither and faither too."

"Do you think there will be more murders at Conall Castle?"

"I don doubt it. Now it's time for me nap. At me age, I needs it."

I rose. "Thank you for the visit, Ewen. Can I come see you again?"

He pointed to the half empty bottle. "Aye. I'll be needin' a refill soon."

I'll be back. Ewen knows more than he is telling me.

CHAPTER FIVE

After leaving the abbey, I hurried back to Conall Castle. By the time I got to lunch in the Great Hall; Noah, Taavi, Martin, and Ruben were finishing their haggis, girolle mushrooms in lobster sauce, and potato scones. I ate a mouthful of haggis, which is a pudding of meat, oatmeal, onions, and spices cooked in a sheep's stomach. I had the strange urge to say, "baaaa."

Noah asked, "Where were you, Nicky?"

"At first, listening in on Brody and Donal," I replied.

Noah's face turned as white as a KKK member. "Are they lovers?"

"Donal would like that," I explained. "But Brody doesn't want to play."

"But Brody played with Barclay."

Why does Noah care about Brody's love life? He doesn't even like him.

Ruben speared a mushroom with his fork. "What does that adorable little Donal see in that big brute Brody?"

Try saying that three times fast.

Martin smirked. "I'll bet people say that about you and me, Ruben."

"Let's give them a reason." Ruben reached for his knife.

I changed the subject. "I also ran into Frazier and Owen."

"Who no doubt haven't a clue," Martin added.

In more ways than one.

Getting his color back, Noah's blue eyes softened. "I think it's sweet how Owen adores Frazier."

"Like Ruben adores me." Martin kissed Ruben's cheek.

I said, "Then I walked over to the abbey and met Mom's leprechaun: the old caretaker at the abbey."

"Did he shed any light on the murders?" my Watson asked.

"Unfortunately, no. But he mentioned that Magnus was in love with another woman before Moira."

Martin was at my side like a dog meeting a generous butcher. "Who?"

"Fenella, a waitress here fifteen years ago. But Magnus's father and Brody's dad intervened, and Fenella married Brody instead. But the moment Lairie was born, Fenella ran away with Balfour, the beefy bartender." *Try saying that three times fast.*

"Let's hear more about *him*." Martin licked his full lips.

Ruben checked his watch. "Time to start shooting again."

"I'm not finished with my lunch."

Ruben stuffed a scone in my mouth. "There. Let's go."

Taavi tugged at my arm. "Can I go with Lairie to the dungeon? She likes to play mistress with me as her slave."

Noah whispered in my ear, "Kink, at Taavi's age?"

I gave Taavi permission and then grabbed a mushroom for the road. As we passed by the buffet, I noticed new laird of the castle Fergus in whispered argument with his fiancé, waiter Hamish.

For the rest of the afternoon, we shot exteriors outside the castle. It was a pleasant task, since the Conall property was truly breathtaking with its rolling emerald hills, golden heather on the meadows, violet moors, turquoise rivers, majestic cliffs, and sparkling sea.

Back in the Great Hall early that evening for dinner with my family and friends, Mom chattered on about her day's sightseeing, while Dad discussed his television watching like a film critic. As Taavi relayed his activities, I couldn't tell whether he was more enamored with Lairie or the castle dungeon. Martin and Ruben continued their usual war of the pink roses. I ate my Scotch lamb with sweet potatoes and then moved on to the apple and bramble dessert, contemplating who killed Barclay and Magnus Conall and why.

When Donal came to our table to ask if everything was all right, Noah asked him, "Where's Brody?"

Why is Noah asking about Brody?

Donal's face lit up like a traffic light. "Brody is in his bedroom with Lairie. He's such a good father. Every night they read together or watch a movie."

"What movie?" Dad asked, devouring the apple and berry pie with vanilla ice cream.

Donal smiled. "Lairie likes action and adventure. Appropriately, Brody likes fantasy."

"Where's Brody room?" Noah asked.

"He and Lairie share a suite in the wing next to yours. It's the first room. Mine's next door. Lairie likes to visit me late at night when she can't sleep. We play computer games and giggle until the wee hours, or until Brody brings her back to their room." Donal grimaced at Fergus standing next to the buffet. "When his royal majesty lets me off, I'll pay them a visit. Lairie will like that." He blinked back tears. "I'm not so sure about Brody."

"Hang in there, Donal," I said.

He squeezed my shoulder. "Thank you, Nicky."

When Donal was gone, I asked Noah, "Why did you ask which room is Brody's?"

"Planning on doing a little sleuthing, Dad?" Taavi asked with a grin.

Noah fidgeted in his chair. "I just wondered where the staff lives."

Martin sipped his hot cocoa. "Have you figured out who the murderer is yet, Nicky?"

I sighed. "Barclay and Magnus weren't exactly popular around here. It seems that everyone wanted them dead."

"Especially the new laird of the castle," Ruben said.

Fergus joined Moira at the next table.

"That's my cue." I excused myself and walked over. Fergus and Moira were dressed in a dark suit and clinging lime cocktail dress. "You both look elegant this evening."

Moira raised her napkin and wiped her dry eyes. "The Chief Inspector won't release Barclay's and Magnus's bodies, so we can't have a funeral."

"So we wanted to honor my brothers tonight, here at dinner," Fergus explained.

Or to celebrate your newfound fortune.

Moira drank her wine. "We miss them both terribly."

I wish there was truth serum in that wine.

Moira acted (badly) concerned. "My psychic said Barclay and Magnus are in the third world, restless, wanting to rest in peace."

Fergus laughed. "Your psychic? Didn't all that go out with the Brahan Seer?"

"Brahan Seer?" I asked.

Fergus motioned for me to take the seat next to him. "The Brahan Seer was a famous teller of the future in seventeenth century Scotland. Only, it was a fairytale. He never existed."

"That's not true." Moira's face turned as red as her hair. "The Brahan Seer told the future. And his descendants still live in Scotland."

Fergus guffawed. "Is your psychic a Brahan then?"

"No." Moira pulled back her bare shoulders. "But the Brahan Seer is proof that some people have the gift, the sixth sense."

That's it! "Moira, how would you like to have a session with a family descended from the Brahan Seer?"

"I would love it! But I don't know any of them."

"*I* do." I smiled like the Cheshire Cat. "As a matter of

fact, I have an in with a Brahan family."

"Who?" Moira asked.

I pointed to my table. "As you know, Scott and Bonnie's ancestors hail from Scotland. What you don't know is they are both direct descendants of the Brahan Seer. And that means Noah has the seer genes too!" *And he looks adorable in them.*

Moira cocked her head. "Scott married someone in his own family?"

I adlibbed, "Noah's mom and dad are distant, very distant relatives. So distant they argue all the time."

Moira seemed unconvinced, but incredibly curious. "Do they see into the future, beyond the fourth wall?"

Isn't that an acting term? "Does a televangelist open Swiss bank accounts?" I reeled her in. "But the Olivers don't like to talk about their powers." I whispered, "They are incredibly shy people."

At the next table, Dad shouted, "Why would I want to visit Rosslyn Chapel? *The Da Vinci Code* is on television tonight!"

I continued. "And they don't seek notoriety."

Noah instructed Taavi, "When we do interviews promoting *this* film, please don't refer to me as a bit player in *your* movie!"

Talking over my family, I said, "I wouldn't ordinarily do this, Moira, but since you have been such a hospitable host to us, I might be able to set up a sitting with you and the Brahans, I mean, the Olivers."

"Could you? *Would* you?" Moira looked more excited than a priest in the altar boys' shower room.

I leaned back in my chair. "I think I can arrange something. Let's meet in the library at nine p.m."

She hugged me, and I smelled lilacs and wine. "Thank you, Nicky! I'll be there!"

After I returned to my table, I swallowed my vitamins and milk thistle capsules with goat's milk. "Mom, Dad, you're getting your wish."

"They're showing the movie *Brave* on TV tonight?" Dad asked.

"You're doing a role-play," I replied. "Noah too. You'll be like a vaudeville family."

"Goody!" Dad kissed the top of Noah's head. "I've been in retirement too long. I better watch *Police Academy* to get ready."

Mom waved her iPhone. "Judy said she wishes she could be a spy like me!"

"Can I role-play too?" Taavi asked.

"No. I'm sorry, son," I replied.

Taavi pouted.

Mom wrapped an arm around his shoulder. "But you'll always be my favorite actor."

"And my favorite grandson." Dad kissed Taavi's forehead.

Ruben said, "You can stay with us this evening, Taavi."

"And watch Ruben snore," Martin added.

After I explained my plan, Noah said, "Mom, Dad, we need to see the costumer, get into makeup, and do some rehearsing."

Martin announced, "Curtain going up on the late show!"

At nine p.m., I led Noah, Mom, and Dad into the library. Highlighting their characters, Mom wore a flowing white dress with a huge crystal pendant dangling from a chain around her neck. Noah and Dad were decked out in white suits. A lavender turban with an amethyst in its center adorned Noah's head, and Dad sported a moonstone on his belt buckle.

Moira was sitting on a tall leather chair next to the massive white stone fireplace.

I said like the host of a television show, "Moira, may I introduce the Oliver family, direct descendants of the Brahan Seer!"

She motioned for us to sit on a leather sofa opposite her. "Of course, I already know Noah."

I shrieked. "Please! His spiritual name is Hona. Calling Hona by that other name might cause him to come out of the trance."

"The trance?" Moira asked.

I nodded. "Prior to a session, the Olivers move into a deep trance."

"How do they do that?"

Not as skilled in improvisation as Noah, I looked to him for help.

Dad replied, "By watching the movie *The Sixth Sense*."

Moira looked skeptical.

Noah added, "And then we chant and breathe with crystals into a deep meditation."

Seeming to accept it, Moira asked, "Have you done sittings with other actors?"

"Of course!" I replied.

"Which ones?" she inquired.

Dad rattled off the names of the cast members he recently saw in old films on television. Moira seemed impressed.

Mom added, "And Judy, Jack, Tommy, Timmy, and Dung."

When Moira looked confused, Noah said, "A new rock group."

I constructed the anagrams in my head. "Tocst will channel his dear ancestor, the Brahan Seer. Nioneb and Hona will channel the great Brahan Seer's wife and son."

"Yes, I will contact the grand seer and permit him to take control of every part of my body." Dad rubbed the stomach protruding over his belt buckle.

"It's ironic that Dad's a seer, since he has cataracts," Mom added.

Noah cleared his throat. "Shall we begin?"

"I'm ready." Moira said.

I removed sage from my jacket pocket, lit it at the fireplace, and waved it around the room. "This is to purify the space." Then I rolled my hips in a circle, hopped on one foot, and threw the sage over my shoulder into the fireplace. "Unfriendly spirits be gone!" Next, I flailed my arms like a seizure victim on a raft down the rapids. "We now summon the great Brahan Seer and his family to visit with us. Break through the barriers of the spirit realm. Use your descendants as a channel to share your wisdom with the still living. Help this questioning widow who so desperately needs your supreme guidance!"

Moira glanced from Noah to Dad to Mom as their bodies collapsed, and then leapt up, shook from side to side, and finally stiffened in their seats.

"I believe the Brahan family is with us now," I said.

Surprisingly, Moira seemed to buy it. "What should I do?"

"Ask a question." I waved my hand as if it were a magic wand.

Moira swallowed hard. "How do I address them?"

I whispered, "'Powerful Brahan Seers' is fine. Or 'Powerful Bra' for short."

"Powerful Brahan Seers, thank you for the audience," Moira said.

At the word "audience," Noah couldn't stop himself from gazing around the room hopefully.

Dad said in a bass Scottish brogue, "We see dead people."

Noah jumped in with a high nasal twang. "And the Brahan Seers see you, lass."

Try saying that three times fast.

"We can see deep, deep into your soul," Noah added.

Without Moira noticing, Mom took a picture of her with the iPhone. Mom sounded like a Scottish televangelist. "Judy believes you are a very troubled woman, I mean, lassie."

"Judy?" Moira asked.

Noah covered with, "That is Jude, the patron saint of psychics."

"The seers share information with the saints," I explained to Moira. "But don't worry about your secrets getting out. The saints keep everything under their wings."

"Ask a question, troubled one." Noah said, "So the seers can see, show, and tell."

"Yes, ask your question," Dad said like the magic mirror in *Snow White*.

Moira slid to the edge of the sofa excitedly. "Will our movie be a hit? Will I win an award? Will I win *all* of the awards?" She licked her lips like a dog next to a freezer during a blackout.

Noah rested his hands on the turban, did a head roll, and then his eyes bulged out like birds in a cuckoo clock. "Your movie will be a resounding success. You will win many awards and thank your acting coach."

Really Noah?

Moira clasped her hands to her chest. "That's wonderful!"

Dad said, "And then a younger actress will work for you, befriend your friends, and steal your next film role."

All About Eve?

Noah spoke over his father, "But you will heed our warning, save your career, and make another movie."

"Will it be successful?" Moira asked.

Noah held out his palms. "Stop! In the name of love."

Come again (no pun intended), Noah?

Noah said, "The seers must ask you a few questions before we can see deeper into your future. You see?"

Moira seemed taken aback. "What is it that you want to know?"

Dad asked, "Tell us, little lassie, how was it that you came to walk on the moors with Heathcliff —"

Wuthering Heights!

Noah interrupted, "How did you come to Conall

Castle?"

Moira pulled her dress over her knees. "My acting work had drie...drained me. So, I applied for a job here as the desk clerk by flir...filing an application with Barclay."

"Then you and the lad Magnus, rather Barclay, Conall became a couple?" Mom said.

Moira sighed. "You were right the first time. Magnus and I got together first, but I thought..." She stopped herself.

"The seers cannot give you a true reading unless you are truthful with them," I said.

Moira nodded. "I thought Barclay would be a better catch...husband for me."

Since he was the oldest son and in line to inherit the castle.

"So, when he proposed, I accepted," Moira said.

Noah asked, "Did Barclay tell you about his wee penchant for lads?"

Moira nodded. "But he promised me that would end at our wedding."

Famous last words.

"But his bi-way didn't go to the highway, did it?" Dad asked.

"No." Moira's face hardened. "Barclay had a... rendezvous with Brody, the head of Housekeeping."

"Which made you angry, jealous, and vengeful," Noah said.

"Actually, it sent me into Magnus's arms," Moira said.

"And you two lived happily ever after," Mom said, as if having finished a romance novel.

"No!" Moira said, "Magnus had loved Fenella, a waitress. Even after Brody married her. And even when Fenella ran off with the bartender, Balfour, fourteen years ago. Magnus never loved me like he loved Fenella. Besides, when Magnus and I were togeth...talking, I found out Magnus was stealing money from Barclay. I didn't know whether to remain loyal to Barclay or Magnus."

"So, you were comforted in the arms of third brother, Fergus," Dad said. "And boy was Fergus surprised when you turned out to be a man."

The Crying Game!

"Fergus! No!" Moira said, "He's engaged to Hamish, our day waiter."

"And during all this, Black Donald has never left the castle's doorstep," Noah said like one of the three witches in *Macbeth*.

Moira seemed to ponder that for the first time. "That's true." She counted off on her manicured fingers. "Barclay's parents, Kendric and Emilia, died in a car accident a year ago. Brody's parents, Elsbeth and Robbie, went down in a plane crash about the same time."

"And the stewardess had to fly the plane," Dad said.

Airport!

Dad asked, "Were Emilia and Elsbeth beautiful lasses, like you?"

Stick to the script, Dad!

Charmed, Moira replied, "They were older than me of course. But aye, Barclay's mother Emilia had stunning red hair and green eyes. Brody's mother Elsbeth was a blonde beauty with piercing blue eyes and a terrific figure, even at her age."

Dad said, "Is that so?"

Mom stepped on Dad's foot.

Continuing, Moira said, "Then of course poor Barclay and Magnus were taken from us. I cried myself to sleep the last two nights."

No doubt because Fergus inherited the castle and not you.

Dad said, "And now each member of your household and staff are in danger, lass, as the murderer might kill you one by one."

And Then There Were None?

"This isn't helping me." Obviously growing impatient, Moira said, "When will you answer my last question? I've answered all of yours!"

"All except one," Noah said. "Did Fergus ever mention his desire to be laird of Conall Castle, even if it meant killing his parents and his brothers?"

Moira nodded. "But I didn't take him seriously." Her hands covered her mouth. "Maybe I should have. Oh, what have I done!" Moira leapt up and hurried to the doorway. "I need to speak to Fergus." She ran back into the room. "Wait! Will I become a movie star?"

Dad replied, "No, but you'll gain notoriety as a reality TV star on an obscure cable television network."

"I'll take it!"

When Moira had gone, I hugged Mom, Dad, and Noah. "Thank you, Oliver family, for a terrific performance!"

Mom kissed my cheek. "Thank *you*, Nicky! It was wonderful to finally act again. I didn't realize how much I missed it." She glanced at her iPhone. "Judy said I'm a natural." She took a selfie and texted. "And that I look like Mata Hari!"

"It felt great being back on the boards," Dad said patting my back.

"You did a terrific job too, handsome husband." I gave Noah a kiss on the cheek.

"I like my reviews." Noah grinned.

Suddenly, Mom swiped at Dad.

"Ow! What's *that* for?" Dad rubbed his shoulder.

"Why did you ask about Emilia and Elsbeth's looks?" Mom said.

"They sounded like attractive older women," Dad replied.

"But you're married!" Mom said.

"And they're dead!" Dad answered.

After their circular argument completed its third circle, Mom and Dad celebrated their successful performances with wine in the library. Exhausted, Noah and I thanked them again and then headed up the long staircase.

When we knocked on the door of Martin and Ruben's

room, we found Ruben sound asleep, and Taavi applying Martin's cold cream facial. After we tucked Taavi into his own bed, Noah and I continued to our room. Faster than a church lobbyist paying off a conservative politician, Noah and I stripped off our clothes at the wardrobe and hoisted ourselves into our huge canopy bed.

I leaned my back against the thick wooden headboard and Noah rested his head on my chest. The room smelled of strawberries.

Noah asked, "You really think the role-play went well?"

"The Olivers will be the next great acting family on Broadway, or the next television psychics."

We shared a long kiss that felt like home. Then Noah placed his head on my shoulder and I ran my fingers through his velvety locks.

"But I'm no closer to figuring this thing out."

Noah replied, "Moira seems to think it's Fergus who is bumping off Conall Castle owners."

"That may be too elementary, my dear Noah. I can't help thinking this runs deeper than three brothers vying for the throne."

"Good point." He sat up cross-legged. "Nicky, don't you think it's a bit of a coincidence that Kendric and Emilia, the Conall brothers' parents, died in a car accident off a cliff a year ago?"

I nodded. "So does Ewan Baird, the abbey caretaker. And I brought it up to Frazier. He reminded me that Brody Naughton's parents died in a plane crash about the same time and they didn't own Conall Castle. Either did Frazier's deceased parents, or any other elderly people who died a natural death in the northern tip of Scotland."

"And that's another thing. Why do people like Hamish and Donal continue working at Conall Castle if they're unhappy here?"

"Hamish is engaged to Fergus, the new laird."

"But the two of them argue constantly over Fergus's late-night disappearances."

"Donal is in love with Brody…for some reason," I said.

"What do you mean?"

"Brody admitted to Donal that he can only make love to a man he doesn't like, and who doesn't like him."

"Brody *said* that?"

I nodded.

Noah seemed miles away.

We snuggled together under the silk sheet. I said, "I know you don't like Brody. If all the gay men in Scotland feel the way you do about him, Brody must have a stable of potential lovers."

Noah hung his head. "I guess I did come on a bit strong with Brody in the Great Hall, and at the staircase."

"I've never seen you so angry."

"He was rude to Lairie and to Donal."

"And they both adore him." I kissed Noah's chin. "And I think Brody adores them too."

"Just like I adore you."

"Right back at you."

We wrapped our arms and legs around each other.

I explained, "I also think Hamish and Donal stay at Conall Castle because they need their jobs. As Frazier said, the castle is one of the few employment opportunities in the northern tip of Scotland."

"Fenella the waitress didn't stay at Conall Castle. She ran off fourteen years ago with Balfour the bartender, leaving Lairie, as a baby, with Brody."

"True."

Noah kissed my sideburn. "Nicky, we know that Moira married Barclay for his position."

No pun intended. "And because Barclay's father, Kendric, pushed him into it. Just like Brody's father, Robbie, pressured Brody to marry Fenella."

"But why did Fenella marry Brody?"

"Why do women marry gay men?"

"Fashion advice?"

We shared a laugh, and another kiss. And another. Then we fell asleep in each other's comforting arms.

I woke in an empty bed with my arms around Noah's pillow. Straining my eyes toward the antique clock on the night table, I realized it was two a.m. After turning on the brass lamp, I rose, and checked Taavi's room. He was sound asleep and alone. Next, I glanced into bathroom. No sign of Noah. So, I stubbed my toe on the wardrobe, put on my robe and slippers, opened the door, and looked both ways. Still no Noah. Yawning and scratching my stomach, I walked down the hall and saw no sign of life. Just then, the first doorway opened in the next wing, and I hid behind a thick wooden column.

In his robe and slippers, Noah exited the room. Brody stood in the doorway with his muscles rippling out of boxers and a T-shirt.

Noah said, "I'm as surprised about this as you are, Brody."

"What do you want to do about it?" Brody asked.

"Let's keep meeting privately until we figure this thing out between us."

"If that's what you want."

"That's what I want."

"Good." Brody cocked his head. "But I thought you didn't like me."

"I don't, however, we need to work this through."

"Are you going to tell Nicky about us?"

"Not unless we know this is real."

I ran back down the hallway into our room and leapt into bed. Moments later, Noah opened the door and joined me. Though we generally cuddle when we sleep, Noah slid to the edge of the bed and lay awake with his eyes wide open. I never fell back to sleep.

CHAPTER SIX

Noah and I woke, showered, and dressed quickly and quietly the next morning. Before we headed into Taavi's room, I asked him, "Did you sleep well?"

Yawning, Noah said, "Not really."

"Me either."

"I'll put ice under my eyes before we shoot the scene today." Noah walked past me.

I grabbed his arm. "Why did you visit Brody last night?"

Noah sat at the foot of the bed. "I woke up in bed and realized I never offered him the Prince Bruce role in the film as we had decided."

I sat next to him. "What did you mean about having to figure things out with him?"

Noah did a doubletake. "Were you listening at Brody's door?"

I feigned indignation. "Of course not. What do you think I am?"

"An amateur sleuth."

Good point. "I was listening from the hallway." It suddenly hit me like a box of Oscars. "As acting coach, you told Brody you'd help him figure things out in the movie. Were you afraid to tell me because he turned down the role?" Leaping to my feet, I paced the room like a father expecting the child antichrist. "Why would I freak out if we don't have a Prince Bruce? It's only the pivotal scene in the movie. And here we are in the most desolate spot in

Scotland with no other options." My throat turned into a boa constrictor. "Did you ask Hamish if he would play Prince Jock, and Donal to be Older Roddy? Did they turn you down too!"

Noah stood and wrapped his arms around me. "Nicky, relax. I'll take care of all the casting today. Concentrate on directing the film." He kissed my Roman nose (which felt out of place in Scotland). "And on loving me."

"Are you sure nothing happened between you and Brody in his room?"

Noah's dimples emerged. "Of course. I'm a one-man man." He kissed my sideburn. "And I don't even like the guy."

He's keeping something from me. I'll let it go. For now.

When Taavi was dressed, we met up with Martin and Ruben and Mom and Dad, and then took the plunge down the long ornate staircase. At the entrance of the Great Hall, Fergus greeted us in his manager's suit. "Good morning, everyone."

Mom said, "Fergus, I'm so sorry about your brothers."

Fergus offered a stiff upper lip (literally since he had been eating porridge). "It has been the worst time of my life."

It was the best of times, it was the worst of times.

"And now you have to run this place all by yourself," Dad said.

"So true."

Is that a twinkle in Fergus's hazel eyes?

"I'll hire more staff before we reopen." Fergus looked away dramatically. "When I'm up to the task."

Always the romantic, Noah said, "I'm sure Hamish will help you."

"Hamish has been a godsend. I don't know what I would do without him." Fergus motioned to Hamish who joined us. "Hamish, please seat our guests at their table."

In his waiter outfit, Hamish whispered to Fergus, "So you remember my name now?"

Fergus whispered back, "What are you talking about?"

Hamish replied in Fergus's ear, "When you got in at three forty-three in the morning, you didn't seem to recognize me. When I helped you into bed, you were babbling something about 'Jack.'"

"That was black jack," Fergus said sotto voce.

After we were seated, Hamish served us orange juice, porridge, and a plate filled with baked beans, mushrooms, sliced ham, a fried egg, a half tomato with cheese, and a potato.

Dad was first to dig in. "This looks terrific. Why don't you make me breakfast like this at home, Mom?"

Mom replied, "Because you'd weigh two hundred and fifty pounds. Fifty pounds more than you weigh now."

Wearing a lime bowtie and sweater vest, Martin ate his porridge. "I'll skip the rest of the food. It's how I stay heart-healthy for longevity."

"You're centuries past longevity, Martin." Ruben spilled a bit of egg on his lime leisure suit. "But you're driving *me* to an early grave."

Martin used his napkin to wipe the egg off his husband's jacket. "You missed an early grave about twenty years ago, Ruben."

Noah looked up at our tall, thin waiter. "Hamish, would you like to play a small role in the last scene of our movie?"

Taavi sized him up. "I approve." Looking cute as usual in a maroon polo shirt and white shorts, our son gave Hamish the hang loose sign.

"You'll play the character of Prince Jock," I explained.

You could have knocked Hamish over with a serving tray. "You want *me* to be in your movie?"

"We sure do," Noah said.

"To play Prince Jock?"

Noah and I nodded.

Hamish laughed wildly. "If the guys in high school

who taunted me for being gay could see me now! Sure. Me in a movie? As Prince Jock! That's amazing! What do I need to know to be an actor?"

How to be a waiter is a good start.

Looking good enough to eat, in a tangerine dress, Mom took a picture and texted. A moment later, she said, "Judy thinks you're photogenic, Hamish, and perfectly cast as royalty."

Who knew Judy was a casting director?

Noah said, "I'll go over everything with you before we shoot the scene, Hamish."

"Great. Thanks. Count me in." Hamish giggled. "Prince Jock! Me, Hamish MacAlastair who was afraid of the bogeyman as a kid. I can't wait to tell Fergus." He hurried off.

In his Hawaiian shirt and Bermuda shorts, Dad said, "I'm glad I got to role-play on this trip too. I think I've been bitten by the acting bug again, Noah."

Mom pinched the vast stomach hanging over Dad's belt. "And there's plenty to bite."

When we finished breakfast, Mom, with Judy's help, announced her sightseeing itinerary for the day and then headed for the front desk. Not being overshadowed, Dad took out his television listing, rattled off his movie viewing plans, and then left for his room. Noah and Taavi went to find our costumer to change into their costumes for the upcoming scene. After I swallowed my vitamins and milk thistle capsules, I headed out of the Great Hall with Martin and Ruben, passing Fergus and Hamish in soft-spoken battle near the buffet.

We walked through the long hallway and headed out of the castle. The three of us enjoyed the beautiful sunny day as we made our way to the stone bridge overlooking the moat. The crew had set up the lights, sound, and camera equipment. The DP instructed the prop mistress to throw fish into the moat, which caused two large snapping alligators, I assumed on loan from a theme park, to make an appearance. The crew filmed them bobbing, weaving, and displaying their molars.

Our costumer led Noah (Oliver), Taavi (Roddy), Fergus (Angus), and Moira (Fiona) to the bridge. The continuity manager held up photographs of their past scenes to ensure their costumes, hair, and makeup were consistent and authentic. As usual, Moira's skin was yanked up under her wig with the headband, and Fergus had gained a few inches from the lifts in his shoes.

Martin went over the dialogue with them, and then Noah offered a number of acting notes. When Ruben looked at his watch and turned the color of the moat water, I called for a rehearsal. After a few times through, we were ready for shooting the long shot.

The scene began with Moira and Fergus kissing on the bridge. I noticed Hamish watching from the edge of the bridge with his arms folded over his chest.

Suddenly, Fergus looked like the Leaning Tower of Pisa, and Moira's face resembled a stroke victim's.

"Cut!"

We waited while Fergus replaced the lift in his right shoe, and Moira reconfigured the headband.

Continuing the scene, Noah and Taavi raced onto the bridge. Noah said, "Ye will pay fer locking this boy up in the secret room!"

Fergus spun toward Noah, tripped over his sword, and landed on the stone floor.

"Cut."

After a crew member helped Fergus to his feet, Fergus continued the scene. "Ye are off yer head, tutor!"

"It were them!" Taavi screamed, pointing at Moira and Fergus. "Me mither and me uncle!"

Moira cornered Taavi at the edge of the bridge. "Ye don want to sass *me*, lad." Her acting training came in handy. In a wild rage, Moira grabbed Taavi by the throat.

"Ye are not my son, lad. Ye dad got hochmagandy with a kitchen wench who spawned you. She's a long time dead, thanks to me."

"Now with me two brothers at Black Donald's side, Fiona and I rule the castle." Fergus glared at Noah. "And no galoots like ye two can stop us!"

Moira went for Taavi's throat. Thanks to Noah's fight choreography, Taavi pulled his arms up quickly, releasing Moira's grasp on him. As she teetered back and forth like a broken umbrella in a storm, Taavi ducked away and pushed at her back.

Our prop person released a mannequin of Moira into the moat, no doubt confusing the alligators.

Fergus raised his sword to Noah. Then, à la Errol Flynn, Noah leapt onto the ledge of the bridge and drew his sword. Fergus joined him on the ledge and they executed a nail-biting swordfight. When Fergus knocked Noah onto his back over the ledge, Noah slipped closer and closer toward the moat. Taavi grasped Noah's fallen sword from the bridge, and stabbed Fergus in the back — releasing the prepacked stage blood underneath Fergus's tunic. Fergus screamed as our prop person unleashed the male mannequin of him into the moat.

"Cut!" I breathed a sigh of relief as the long shot was completed successfully — without anyone really getting killed.

We repeated the scene with close-ups on each of the four actors. In Fergus's close-up, the blood-pack malfunctioned. Taavi had to stab, punch, kick, and bite at Fergus's back until Fergus finally bled. Moira's face fell so many times during her close-up that she finally crazy-glued her face to the wig.

By the time we finished shooting, it was way past lunchtime. So, Hamish served us lunch on the bridge. After he distributed cloth napkins and silverware, he gave each of us a small shepherd's pie and a cup of ale (except for

Taavi).

As Noah, Taavi, and I sat on the ledge where Noah (as Oliver) nearly met his death, Fergus and Hamish stood on the opposite side of the bridge in heated discussion.

Fergus raised his long nose up toward Hamish's button nose. "I said no, Hamish."

"Why?"

"Because my brother was right. It would cost too much money."

Hamish groaned. "The staff can do the renovations."

"It would take a lot more than our skeleton staff to bring that old ballroom back to life. The curtains are frayed and worn. The chandeliers are tarnished. And the floor is cracked and unsafe."

"Fergus, please!"

"We don't have the money, Hamish."

Hamish replied under his breath, "And we both know why."

Why? Why?

Fergus placed an arm around his fiancé. "Now that I own the castle, once we open for business again, we'll be back on our feet soon enough." He kissed Hamish's cheek. "And we can get married in any of the other castle rooms."

"It's not the same." Hamish blinked back tears. "The ballroom is a special place."

Fergus sat on the ledge. "How about if we get married on the cliff overlooking the sea? It's beautiful there."

Hamish sat next to him. "It's also where Barclay fell to his death. Are you that insensitive, Fergus?"

I'll go with "yes" for the win.

Fergus scratched at his red hair. "How about down at the lake? It's a peaceful and pretty setting."

"You know I don't like lakes."

"Because of some dreams you had as a wee boy?"

Hamish rubbed his forehead. "I had those dreams every night as a lad."

"Each dream was the same?"

Hamish nodded. "The Shellycoat bogeyman rattled toward me when I was swimming in a river."

Fergus grinned. "Your mother must have read you a story."

"Aye, but those dreams seemed real to me."

"The bogeyman covered in seashells, haunting rivers and streams, is a Scottish myth."

"Then why did I dream about him every night?" Hamish looked away. "And why does the bogeyman still plague my dreams now?"

Role-play number three!

Fergus asked, "Is that why you wake up screaming in the night? You dream about the bogeyman?"

"As if you care, the hour you get back."

Fergus kissed his cheek. "You know I love you, Hamish."

"Do you, Fergus? Do you really? Sometimes I wonder." Hamish ran away.

I followed him into the castle lobby. "Hamish!"

He turned back to face me with tears streaming down his rosy cheeks.

"I accidentally (*totally on purpose*) overheard what you said to Fergus about your childhood fear of the Shellycoat bogeyman."

Hamish wiped his face with the cuff of his white shirt. "Are you going to mock me too?"

"No. Quite the opposite. Hamish, I had the same dreams and the same fears...until I came to Conall Castle — where I met the bogeyman."

Hamish did a doubletake. "The Shellycoat bogeyman is a myth."

"I saw him, Hamish."

"Are you sure?"

I nodded like a ragdoll in a spaceship.

"Where?"

"At the lake." I painted the picture with my words. "As the sun was setting magenta, azure, and honeysuckle over the violet moors, there he was."

Hamish looked as if he had seen a ghost—or a bogeyman. "What happened?"

"My heart raced in my chest. I couldn't breathe. I thought I was about to meet my maker." I added like a children's television show host, "But do you know what I did?"

Transfixed, Hamish shook his head.

"I confronted him. I asked the Shellycoat bogeyman why he plagues my dreams. And what he wanted from me."

"What did he say?"

"He asked me some questions. I answered them. Then I walked back to the castle. And I never had the dream again."

Hamish sat on a leather bench. "Do you think if *I* talked to the bogeyman and answered his questions, my nightmares would finally stop?"

I sat next to him. "I think it's worth a try."

"What should I do?"

"At sunset, make your way down to the lake. Stand at the edge and call out, 'Shellycoat bogeyman!'"

Hamish covered his face with his hands. "I've feared the bogeyman my entire life. I don't think I can do that."

"I think you can." Resting a hand on his shoulder, I said, "And won't it all be worth it when you never have another nightmare?"

He nodded.

I squeezed his shoulder, left Hamish, and found my film crew outside. We took a few more shots of the snapping alligators and then wrapped for the day.

As we entered the castle lobby, Martin and Ruben headed to the library with Martin shouting, "Since you never talk to me anymore, Ruben, at least I'll have the comfort of a good book while you snore."

"I don't snore," Ruben exclaimed.

"Right. And anti-gay politicians don't cruise public men's rooms."

When they were gone, Lairie pranced down the stairs in a long, flowing robe, and greeted Noah, Taavi, and me. "I am Lairie, the mistress of the castle. How may I help you lads?"

Before we could reply, Brody was at Lairie's side like a guard dog. "Leave the folks alone now, Lairie."

"Lairie isn't bothering us," Noah said.

"Can Lairie and I play in the dungeon again?" Taavi asked like a dungeon master.

"Only if you stay close to Lairie," Noah said.

With his beard and jeans, Brody looked every bit the housekeeper. "Sorry, Lairie has to help me test the smoke detectors in the rooms."

"Can't we do that later, Dad?" Lairie asked with Taavi's familiar whine.

Donal came down the stairs in his waiter attire. "I'll help you test the alarms tomorrow, Brody. Let Lairie play with Taavi."

Brody's pectoral muscles swelled under his sweatshirt and the veins in his strong hands expanded. "You aren't helping, Donal."

"Neither are you," Donal replied next to Brody. "Lairie's a lass. She needs to have some fun."

"She has plenty of fun. I see to that. Right now, she has work to do."

"Why do you get to make every decision...for all of us?"

Brody glared down at Donal. "I only make decisions for my daughter and me."

Donal turned away so Brody wouldn't see the tears brimming in his soft blue eyes.

"Donal didn't mean any harm, Dad." Lairie moved

next to Taavi. "I'm sorry we can't play today. I have to slave for the tyrannical Fergus and Moira."

"It's all right." Taavi smiled at her consolingly. "We can play another day."

Noah made his way between Brody and Donal. "We won't be here for much longer, Brody. I don't see why the children can't enjoy each other's company."

"I explained why," Brody said. "Do you have a hearing problem?"

Donal turned on Brody. "Don't take things out on Noah."

Lairie added, "And don't take things out on Donal, Dad."

"Donal needs to get to work in the Great Hall." Brody smirked at Noah. "And Noah and I have some unfinished business. Don't we Noah?"

Noah nodded.

"Until then." Brody took Lairie's hand and pulled her up the stairs.

Noah and Taavi started up after them.

I called out, "I'll be back in a minute." I followed Donal down the hallway and stopped him near the entrance to the Great Hall. "Can we talk?"

Donal glanced at his watch. "I'm on duty in five minutes."

"Five minutes it is." I led Donal to the window seat at the nearby turret. "What are your future goals, Donal?" *I sound like a teenager's father interrogating her first date.*

Donal looked more ambitious than a conservative politician meeting a SuperPac CEO. "I'd like to manage a restaurant someday."

"With Fergus inheriting Conall Castle, I hear he's seeking a replacement for restaurant manager."

Donal laughed. "It won't be me. It'll be Hamish. Fergus thinks I'm lazy and incompetent." He shrugged. "Takes one to know one, I guess."

"You're a fine waiter, Donal."

"And that's all I'll ever be around here."

"Speaking of jobs, did Noah speak to you about playing Older Roddy in our movie?"

"Yes." Donal smiled. "And I ran into Taavi and the costumer earlier today. Your son said I was his choice to play him as a grownup. I was flattered." He sighed. "Though I don't feel very much like a grownup lately."

"You'll be fine. It's a small role at the end of the movie."

"I've never acted before."

"Noah will help you."

"Noah's a terrific guy. I really like his parents too. And, like Lairie, I'm wild about Taavi."

How about me? Am I chopped Scottish liver? "So, are you game to join us on the movie?"

Donal took my hand. "Consider me a cast member."

After we shook on it, I said, "You'll be playing opposite Brody."

Donal gazed at the stone floor. "Brody won't like that."

"I have the feeling Brody will like that just fine."

Donal's eyes met mine. "When I hear Fergus and Hamish discussing their wedding plans, I can't help feeling envious. I wish…" His voice trailed off.

Practicing for when Taavi grows older, I said, "Donal, people come to love in different ways, at different times. Sometimes love is elusive. Other times it hits us over the head. But don't ever give up on love, because there's one thing that's for certain. Love always wins."

He hugged me and then disappeared into the Great Hall.

I walked over to the library, where I found Martin and Ruben sitting on high back leather chairs next to the tall stone fireplace. Sipping hot cocoa from china cups, they offered me their favorite drink. I sat across from them, placed a cloth napkin on my lap, gazed at the low fire, and drank the sweet hot drink.

After a few minutes, Martin asked, "Have you figured it all out yet, Nicky?"

"Not exactly."

"Pretend we're back at Treemeadow, and use us as a sounding board," Martin said.

"Who benefits most from Barclay's and Magnus's deaths, and from their parents' deaths before them?" I tented my fingers. "Fergus becomes the new laird of the castle. Brody gets his revenge on the Conalls for refusing his parents' burial in the Conall cemetery, and he no longer has a tyrant for a boss. But Moira loses her lover and her position as mistress of the castle. And Donal simply trades in an unsupportive manager for an unsupportive owner. And then there is Hamish."

Ruben patted my knee. "It sounds like you need to do some more investigating."

"And to do another role-play," Martin added.

"I think you're both right." I sighed. "This is a complicated case."

"As were all of them," Martin replied. "And you solved each one."

"I hope I still have the stuff," I said.

Martin seemed to grow six inches in his chair. "Nicky Abbondanza, you are the best armchair detective there is."

Slumping in my chair, I said, "I don't feel like it."

"Well you should." Martin added, "And do you know why?"

I shook my head.

"Because you use the art of drama to catch your killers!" Martin's words were hypnotic. "Think about the plot, theme, and characters. Listen to their dialogue. Take note of what they *don't* say. Observe their actions and motivations. Identify their objectives and uncover the obstacles to their goals."

As if someone who was healed at a tent revival

meeting, I said, "Yes, Martin, I am ready to use my theatre skills to once again catch a killer!"

Martin rose from his chair with fervor. "The curtain is going up on the killer, Nicky. Shine your spotlight. Fly in the set. Begin the overture. And brace yourself for the applause!"

I leapt to my feet, ready to face my appreciative audience, waiting to hear "Bravo!"

However, Noah, Taavi, Mom, and Dad stood in front of me.

"Dinnertime," Dad said, patting his bulbous stomach.

Ruben rested his cup on an antique end table and tapped at his watch. "Yes, my bedtime is approaching, Nicky."

Back to reality.

We walked down the hallway, entered the Great Hall, and Fergus seated us at our usual table near the large stone fireplace. Two seconds after we were seated, Fergus shouted, "Donal, stop dawdling and see to our guests!"

Donal served us Scottish trout, tomato couscous, fennel salad, and pumpkin crumble with sweet mint iced tea.

Mom took a picture of the table and texted. "Judy said this is a feast for a king in a castle. *(That was a big leap, Judy.)* And she thinks you are the cutest little thing, Donal."

Donal blew Mom a kiss and she giggled like a young girl meeting a movie star. Then looking down at her dessert, Mom said, "I make pumpkin crumble too."

"Not like this you don't." Dad started his meal off with the huge dollop of whipped cream on the spicy dessert.

Donal came to Mom's rescue (before she could empty her iced tea on Dad's bald head). "I'm sure your crumble is even better than this one, Mrs. Oliver."

"Thank you, Donal." Mom winked at him. "Call me, Bonnie."

Is Mom flirting with the waiter?

"And 'Bonnie' is the perfect name for such a beautiful woman." Donal grinned.

Eating it up (no pun intended), Mom replied, "And you are a sweet young man. Inside and out. Brody is foolish not to notice that."

Donal's cheeks reddened.

"Leave Brody alone, Mom," Dad said.

Tearing into his trout, Martin happily joined the gossip bandwagon. "Are you and Brody an item then, Donal?"

He shrugged. "I wish I knew." Donal smiled. "Actually, I wish I was with the man I loved for forty years, like the two of you."

"Careful what you wish for," Ruben replied.

"You would die without me," Martin exclaimed, eating Ruben's salad.

"Yes," Ruben said. "A peaceful death."

After Donal left, Taavi drew the attention to himself (a family trait). "How did my scenes go today, Dad?"

Noah kissed Taavi, and then wiped couscous off the boy's cheek. "You were terrific, son, brimming with emotion, and fearless in your acting choices."

"I had a good teacher," Taavi said to Noah's delight.

"I'm really proud of you both," I added.

Mom and Dad raised their glasses. "Here, here!"

As if he were ninety years old and retiring, Taavi said, "After my last scene is shot tomorrow, I'll miss acting."

Noah rested a hand on his shoulder. "There will be more roles for you, young man."

As his Brahan Seer character, Dad said, "I see an Oscar in your future."

"And a Tony and an Emmy," Mom added in psychic wonder.

"I'd like to do a role-play and solve this case." Taavi cleared his throat in my direction.

"That reminds me! I'm doing a role-play tonight." I filled them in on my plan to question Hamish at the lake.

Everyone wished me luck.

Then Mom told us all about her sightseeing — displaying more pictures than the Louvre. Dad was next, offering his review of *National Lampoon's Vacation* and *European Vacation*.

After downing my vitamins and milk thistle, I left Taavi with Mom and Dad, and then Noah and I searched for the costumer.

Later that evening, Noah hid behind a grassy knoll and I stood near the lake. I heard Noah giggle at my muddy hair, hands, face, and feet, as well as my leotard and tights — covered with seashells. I took a step toward the lip of the lake and the shells rattled like maracas on a roller coaster.

Hamish appeared at the opposite side of the lake.

"Boo!"

"Ahhhhh!"

I laughed. "I'm just playing with you, sonny."

He asked in a voice that shook more than an intoxicated flight attendant during turbulence. "Are you the Shellycoat bogeyman?"

Either that or I have a strange fetish for seashells. I was going for Dracula, but what came out was a combination of Yiddish and Polish. "Sure, I'm the bogeyman of the loch. Who else would I be with mud all over my body and seashells dangling off me like gold jewelry?"

"I thought you were a legend."

"I am. In my own mind." I let out a harrowing guffaw.

Hamish took in a deep breath and then said, "Why do you terrorize me in my dreams?"

"I'm the bogeyman. What, do you expect me to meet you for brunch?"

Summoning up his courage, Hamish asked, "How can I get you to stop?"

I took a step forward and three shells fell off my leotard. "Let's have a chat."

"Why?"

"You rather I go back to scaring you?"

"No, but I don't understand."

"The thing is, I don't have many friends. Being a bogeyman doesn't exactly make me A-list, sonny." More shells dropped off. "So, tell me all about yourself or I go back to the 'boo' routine."

"If I tell you about myself, will you stop haunting my dreams?"

"Tell you what I'll do. Answer my questions honestly, and I will plague your dreams no more. I'll even sell you some seashells at discount." *Try saying that three times fast.* More shells slid off.

"What do you want to know?"

Sounding like a matchmaker, I said, "So tell me, are you single?"

Hamish ran a hand through his brown locks. "Why do you want to know *that*?"

"It gets lonely in the marshes. Maybe I want to live my life vicariously through yours."

"You wouldn't want *my* life."

"What could be worse than looking at nothing but fish and seaweed all day, and spooking nice people in their wet dreams each night (*no pun intended*)? Not to mention these itchy seashells."

Hamish sighed. "I'm having some trouble with my fiancé."

"Trouble in castle paradise?"

Hamish seemed to forget he was talking to the villain of his childhood nightmares as he became immersed in his own drama. "I love Fergus, and I thought he loved me."

"Thought?"

Hamish nodded. "We met when I applied for my job as a waiter at the castle. Fergus was my manager. He and I fell instantly in love."

"But?"

"I realized he has a problem."

"Tell the bogeyman all about it, so I can make it better. Does he need a recommendation for a good fish to eat in a restaurant? Want me to visit someone bothering him and infiltrate his dreams with a good falling-off-a-cliff nightmare? Need to decorate a box with seashells as a gift?"

Noah threw a pebble at me. More shells fell off. I was beginning to look like a dirty ballet dancer doing *Swan Lake*.

"I don't think you can fix this," Hamish said.

"This?"

"Fergus is addicted to gambling." He rubbed his button nose. "And to sex with other guys."

"You're right. That I can't fix." *So that's where Fergus goes every evening.* I stepped on a seashell and screamed. "Sorry, I was empathizing with your situation."

Tears filled Hamish's brown eyes. "I know it's insane. But I still love him."

And you still want to co-own the castle. "Let's take this one addiction at a time. Where does Fergus get the green stuff, and I don't mean seaweed, to feed his gambling habit?"

"Fergus spent the money his parents left him." Hamish looked down at the grass. "He also stole from the hotel intake." The tears slid down his cheeks. "And he emptied my bank account."

"And his brothers didn't fire him? You didn't kill him?"

"His sister-in-law, Moira, covered for him. Just like she protected Fergus's brother Magnus when he stole from the hotel."

"Why would she do that?"

"I guess to stay on the good side of whoever owns the castle."

"Your life is worse than the nightmares I give people,

where they leave the house undressed in the morning. You sure you want to marry this guy, sonny?"

Hamish banged his hands against the sides of his head. "Not if Fergus continues acting like a spoiled child."

"Have you two talked about this, sonny?"

"Constantly."

"Maybe it's time to stop talking and start offering Fergus an ultimatum."

"You're right!"

"I could terrorize his dreams for you? I've got a few horror stories that would make him gasp and choke like an apnea patient on his back after eating a full meal."

"No need." He started off.

"Where are you going?"

"To have this out with Fergus once and for all. Even if it kills one of us."

That's never good to say in my presence.

When the coast was clear, Noah came out (no pun intended) of hiding. "Don't you think that was a bit over the top, Nicky?"

"I uncovered Hamish's secrets, didn't I? Ow!" After stepping on another shell, I pulled off my leotard and tights. Noah handed me a wipe from his bag and I cleaned off my face and hands. When I reached for my clothes, Noah hid the bag behind his back. "What are you doing?"

Noah had a devilish look in his crystal blue eyes. "I don't know, Nicky. What am I doing?" He yanked off his clothes and then pressed his body against mine. As he ran his soft hands down the muscles in my back, I cupped his round bottom and we shared a kiss.

"What if someone is watching?"

Noah giggled. "Nobody's watching, except the bogeyman." He whispered in my ear, "And I think the bogeyman is incredibly sexy."

We kissed under the moonlight. Then Noah pulled me down and we sat on the muddy grass next to the lake. *Our first time having dirty sex.* Since I know Noah loves it (and I like it too), I flexed my pecs and biceps as he kissed and squeezed them. When he got to my abs, I lay back and rested my head (the big one, well, the bigger one) on a small bush (not what you're thinking). Noah tugged on my pubic hair with his lips and then tickled my sacs with the tip of his tongue. When I crooned in appreciation, he kissed little Nicky, or should I say big Nicky. Stretching open his mouth as much as possible, he went to work. I ran my fingers through his silky blond curls and moaned in delight. "I love you so much."

"You're my love, my life, and my joy."

I mounted him from behind and wrapped my arms around his smooth chest. As I flicked at his firm nipples, he cried out in joy. I pressed my torso against his, laying him onto his stomach. *I hope there aren't ticks in Scotland.* Then I kissed his back and finally buried my nose in Noah's hair, smelling strawberries.

"I want you, Nicky."

"You've got me, forever." I gently slid inside him.

He cried out from my girth, and in anticipation of what was to come. After we built up a steady rhythm, I grabbed on to him and rubbed. Minutes later, we both screamed our pleasure as I filled Noah with my love, and he left his mark on the grass beneath us. I caught my breath and turned Noah around to face me.

He kissed the cleft in my chin. "You mean everything to me."

"You're all mine." I kissed his soft neck. "We're Nicky and Noah forever."

"Forever."

After more kissing, we got to our feet and put on our clothes. I picked up the bogeyman costume to return to our costumer, and Noah and I headed back to the castle. It was a romantic walk under the starry sky, past the lake, and through the meadow.

When we arrived at the long stone bridge to the castle, Noah pointed at the moat beneath us. I stared down at the two alligators, snapping their jaws and exposing their teeth.

"Nicky, look!"

Below the water's surface was Moira's leg, followed by Fergus's arm.

"Do you think it's the mannequins?" Noah asked.

"Mannequins don't bleed."

The alligators seemed to nod as they lowered themselves back into the water. *Snap!*

CHAPTER SEVEN

The next morning, the buffet in the Great Hall was set with yogurt, fruit, whole grain toast, cereal, milk, and orange juice. Our crew and hotel workers filed in and out between interviews with Chief Inspector Lennox Frazier in the library. Since Noah and I had found the bodies (technically, the alligators had found them before us), Frazier and Owen had already interviewed us the night before. The two dead bodies were so maimed by the alligators, I suspected they would provide no forensic clues. My inner Sherlock Holmes was tickled when the chief inspector asked me to sit in again on the morning interviews. So I did—after I downed my vitamins and milk thistle capsules.

Since the murders occurred late at night, none of the staff had seen or heard anything. Martin used his interview with Frazier to complain about "Ruben snoring like a narcoleptic ape using a chain saw." Ruben countered in his interview by pontificating on "Martin's nightly facial cream, which smelled like a men's locker room inhabited by skunks, rotten eggs, and sewage." Taavi asked the confused chief inspector if he and Owen act out role-plays to catch murderers. Mom took a picture of Frazier and Owen, thereby announcing Judy's decision that the two officers make a lovely couple. Dad recommended that the inspectors watch *Beverly Hills Cops*.

Frazier stretched his legs between interviews and knocked over a coatrack which crashed into a bookcase that toppled over onto a grandfather clock. "Sorry."

Owen righted the bulky pole (*it's not what you're thinking*), bookcase, and clock. "No harm done, Lennox, I mean, Chief Inspector. Would you like me to bring in the next suspect, I mean, interview?"

"Give Nicky and me a few moments will you, Owen, ah, Inspector Steward?"

"Of course." The tall, thin man stood at the library door like a frame.

"On the other side of the doorway, please."

"Right. I knew that, sir." Owen left the room and closed the heavy wooden door behind him.

Frazier walked over to the large stone fireplace, knocked into the poker, replaced it, and then tipped over the stand, sending all the tools sprawling onto the stone floor. "Sorry."

Feeling like Owen, I rose and righted the stand and gathered the tools. "How do you think the interviews are going?"

Frazier yanked out the notepad and ripped his suit jacket pocket. "I've got quite a few clues. My father, the ex-Chief Superintendent, would be proud."

Or rather turning over in his grave. I leaned on the fireplace mantel à la Holmes. "What are your clues?"

He glanced through the pages of the notepad. "Four victims. All in the same family. No one among the living knows anything."

Not exactly an impressive list of clues.

Sitting back behind the desk (and tipping over the tall leather chair), the bulky man said, "I have a suspicion the murderer is copying your movie." He rose from the floor. "I think you'd better stop production."

I bent down on my knees in front of him. (Wrong again.) "Please, Frazier. We only have a few more scenes to shoot." Channeling Moira, I added, "Let us finish the film to honor the deceased."

He scratched at his square chin and his elbow knocked

over a paperweight. "It's just a few more scenes, you say?"

I nodded like a buoy in the storm of the century.

"Then I suppose it's all right."

I breathed a sigh of relief. "Thank you, Frazier."

"But in return, I'd like to know your hunch about the identity of our murderer."

Taking on my Sherlock Holmes persona, I jumped up and paced the room. "I've narrowed it down to four suspects: Brody Naughton, Lairie Naughton, Donal Blair, and Hamish MacAlastair."

Frazier sat. Having never righted the chair, he went crashing to the floor. "How do you know they are the prime suspects?"

I tapped my temple. "The little gray cells told me. And my inquisitive nature." *Not to mention the other possible suspects have been murdered.*

"Why do you suspect them?" Frazier rose behind the desk and accidentally jabbed a pen into his palm. "Ouch!"

I handed him my handkerchief. "You'll see when I, I mean, *we* interview them. Please keep in mind that any of them could have been on the bridge last night."

Owen peeked his head inside the library. "Are you ready for the next interview, Le…Chief Inspector?"

I replied, "Yes, I am, Inspector Steward. Please send him in." I reset Frazier's chair and sat next to him. "Watch and learn."

Brody entered the room looking like a lumberjack in a flannel shirt, jeans, and boots. He slouched down in the tall leather chair opposite the desk. "I didn't see anything. And neither did my daughter."

I stood and leaned against the desk like a television attorney in a hushed studio courtroom. "Brody, isn't it true that you were miffed at Barclay Conall for his 'slam, bam, thank you, man' routine with you?"

Looking like a conservative politician being confronted with evidence of global warming, Brody practically growled at me. "The termination of my relationship with Barclay was mutually agreed upon."

I sat on the desk. "And aren't you enraged that your parents, Elsbeth and Robbie Naughton, after spending their lives working for the Conalls, were not buried in the Conall cemetery along with Kendric and Emilia Conall? And wasn't your rage directed toward the very people who prevented that burial: Barclay and Magnus Conall?"

Brody said behind gritted teeth, "Kendric and Emilia were buried there. My folks should have been too. They worked hard for the Conalls their whole lives."

Frazier raised his hand, knocking over a pencil holder, which sent pencils rolling across the desk. "I can bear witness to that."

Is he the chief inspector or a character witness for Brody?

"Kendric Conall kept my mother working long hours in the office." Frazier gathered the pencils and put them back.

"He did the same with my mother in Housekeeping, and my dad as caretaker outside." Brody tugged at his beard so hard I thought it might tear out of his skin. "And Fergus Conall worked my ex-wife Fenella the same way in the restaurant." He looked away. "Before she ran off with Balfour the bartender years back."

"And that made you want to kill everyone who bore the Conall name," I said.

Brody did a doubletake. "No! I didn't kill anyone." He pounded his fist into his palm. "But I sure thought about it."

Frazier applauded my performance. "Well done, Nicky!"

I bowed.

Then Frazier cleared his throat. "Ah, that's all we need for now, Brody."

Lairie was next, still wearing her long white robe.

Standing over the fourteen-year-old, I said, "Back in

the states, our juvenile prisons are full of girls like you who covet what others own."

"What does 'covet' mean?" she asked Frazier.

He shrugged.

"I'll redirect." Leaning over her, I said, "Why do you pretend to be mistress of this castle?"

Her blue eyes widened. "Because it's fun."

"And because you despise the Conalls, the *real* owners of the castle?"

"Yes. They are selfish brutes."

"And that is why *you* took their lives!"

She giggled. "Are we acting in a scene?" She explained to Frazier, "I acted in the movie. It was so cool!"

Frazier whispered to me, "I think you're barking up the wrong juvenile."

"Witness released — for now."

Donal took the hot seat next.

I sat behind the desk. "You had good reason to kill the Conalls, Donal."

"I did?" Donal asked.

"You were jealous of Brody's past relationship with Barclay. And you wanted Fergus's position as restaurant manager."

His angelic face saddened. "Brody is responsible for breaking my heart, Nicky. And *he's* still alive."

"The lad has a point," Frazier said.

You're not helping!

Finally, Hamish sat before us.

Frazier said, "I'm sorry for your loss, Hamish."

Hamish wiped a tear off his cheek. "I think I'm still in shock."

"Let me bring you back to reality." I paced over to the fireplace. "We know that Barclay and Magnus stood in the way of your fiancé inheriting the castle. And we are also aware that Fergus cheated on you and stole your money."

"Since you know everything, why ask me any

questions?" Hamish sneered.

"I only have one question for you, Hamish." I leaned in for my close-up. "With your fiancé deceased, who inherits the Conall Castle and all the property around it?"

"I do. It was in Hamish's will."

Frazier made a note on his pad, tried to place it inside his ripped jacket pocket, and the notepad fell to the floor. He bent over to pick it up and banged his head on the desk.

"Thank you for your honesty, Hamish." I grinned. "We will remember your testimony."

With the interviews completed, I met up with my family at the Great Hall buffet for lunch—Scottish pie, meaning minced mutton. Hungry yet? Then Noah and Taavi rushed off to change into their costumes for the next scene. I wished Mom a good afternoon of sightseeing and Dad an enjoyable time watching *The Accidental Tourist* in his room.

Next, I made my way around various corridors to the castle room, where I found our crew members set up and taking orders from the DP. Ruben, in a chartreuse leisure suit, whispered in my ear, "Let's shoot this before anyone else gets killed."

In a chartreuse bowtie and sweater vest, Martin was at Ruben's side. "Stop overreacting as usual, Ruben. Nobody is going to get killed here."

Ruben glared at his husband. "I wouldn't be so sure."

Noah (Oliver) and Taavi (Roddy) arrived in their historical costumes.

I called for quiet and joined Martin and Ruben behind our camera operator. We rehearsed the scene in the stunning room laden with a giant hand-carved canopy bed, enormous oak desk, and various leather chairs. It was the first of a montage of scenes highlighting Roddy and Oliver enjoying their lives as young laird and his top advisor. We shot the scene quickly without a hitch, except for Taavi leaning into the camera and nudging Noah away during

Noah's close-up.

"Let's move on to the next shot." Ruben's eyes seemed permanently glued to his watch.

Martin said, "I think I'll nickname you Big Ben."

Ruben giggled naughtily. "Is that your new pet name for me, lover?"

Martin laughed uproariously. "Hardly."

We continued shooting the montage with Taavi and Noah celebrating in the Great Hall and library. The scenes went fine, except for Frazier's clumsiness apparently rubbing off on the cast. Taavi's sporran got caught on the fireplace poker in the Great Hall, which landed him head-first inside the large stone fireplace. Thankfully unharmed, Taavi got to his feet met by applause from the crew. "I was smoking hot in that scene, Pop!"

There was also a little mishap in the library when Noah rose from behind the desk and a bronze desk knob caught hold of his kilt, rendering Noah "on library display."

Then we all headed out of the castle to the van, which drove us to the moors. The crew set up for the next scene, where Taavi and Noah run laughing through the moors, excited by their newfound freedom. The moment the crew was ready, Ruben leapt up and down like a barefoot swami on hot stones. "Hurry up and shoot the scene before we lose the light!"

Martin stood next to him on the large rock. "There is plenty of light. Your cataracts are blocking out the sun, Ruben."

"I thought they only blocked out *you*." Ruben kissed Martin's cheek.

We shot without a rehearsal. All went well until Noah's cloak got caught in a tree branch and Taavi's brogue picked up a stone—sending my husband and son dangerously close to the cliff's edge. I called, "Cut," and rescued my family. Then we reshot the scene successfully, and finally drove in the van back to the castle.

Upon entering, Noah and Taavi hurried upstairs to change into their own clothes. I raced down the hall, pilfered a bottle of whiskey, backtracked outside, and took a brisk walk across the bridge and over the cobblestone path to the abbey. After running up the steps and yanking open the heavy door (realizing I needed to get back to the gym at Treemeadow), I passed through the abbey entryway. As my eyes adjusted to the lack of light, I heard a soft whimpering. "Ewan?"

The old man appeared at the entrance to the worship area. After wiping his face with his sleeve, he aimed bleary hazel eyes in my direction. "I can use that about now, lad."

I offered him the bottle and he drank long and hardy. Then he sat on a stone bench. I rested next to him. "You're Fergus's father, aren't you?"

He nodded. "You a detective, lad?"

"Something like that."

He drank some more. After wiping his mouth with his beard, he asked, "How did ye know?"

"On my last visit, you mentioned that Emilia and Kendric Conall had secrets from each other. And that Kendric spent his time working in the office, and Emilia visited the abbey. After seeing your reaction to Fergus's death just now, I realized Emilia came to the abbey to see *you*."

Tears brimmed his eyes. "Emilia were a fine woman, sweet, kind, with skin fair as sheep's wool, hair as gold as heather, and cheeks rosy as a sunset. After Barclay and Magnus were born, Kendric lost interest in Emilia. One day she visited me here and we got to haver about this, that, and everythin'." He chuckled. "And she asked me to reel dance with her, since Kendric wouldn't. So, I did. She visited me every day after that one. We talked, laughed, danced and..." He looked away.

"Did Kendric know you were Fergus's father?"

"Aye. But he swore Emilia to secrecy."

"So, Fergus didn't know either?"

He shook his head and gray hair flew off in every direction. "Emilia wouldn't let me tell the lad. After the car accident, I spoke the truth, but Fergus didn't believe me, or he didn't *want* to believe me." The craters and crevices on his face deepened. "Fergus called me a liar and a drunk."

It takes one to know one.

After a long swig, he said, "I know Fergus drank, gambled, stole, and he were crabbit to the workers and to Hamish too. But Barclay were crabbit to the workers also, and Mangus stole too." As if trying to convince himself more than me, he said, "And I know Fergus whored around with lads in the abbey. But so did Barclay with Brody, and Mangus with Fenella and later with Moira. And afore that, I caught Brody's mither, Elsbeth, in here with a lad when she were a young maid. And as I said, I met up with Emilia Conall meself. So I can't be agin me own son fer doin' it, can I?"

A father's blind love. I rested a hand on his bony shoulder. "I'm sorry for your loss, Ewan."

He looked up at me with tears rolling down the craters of his cheeks onto his long beard. "That means a lot to me, laddie."

"I wish you could have been a father to your son."

"I'd have been a better faither than Kendric Conall, who ne'er saw outside his office, and was mean as a tiger."

I rested back on the bench. "The workers at Conall Castle who I spoke with complained about Barclay, Mangus, and Fergus as their boss."

"And they'll blether about Hamish too." He stared out the stained-glass window. "Power is a dangerous thing to have, lad. I don't envy Hamish."

"Ewan, do you think Hamish's life is in danger?"

He took a long drink and seemed to ponder my question. "If it isn't, that marks Hamish as the murderer, don't it?"

"I wish I knew." I thanked Ewan for his time, patted him on his skeletal back, and left the abbey.

Minutes later, I met my family and friends at the Great Hall for dinner. Hamish, out of his waiter clothes and wearing a dark suit, greeted us at the doorway. "Welcome to my restaurant." Then he shouted, "Donal! Stop mooning over Brody and take care of our guests!"

In his waiter's outfit, Donal seated us at our usual table next to the vast stone fireplace. Looking summery in her canary dress, Mom patted Donal's arm. "We still think you're the best waiter at Conall Castle."

Donal sighed. "Hamish would disagree with you."

Overhearing from the buffet, Hamish said, "You won't be a waiter here for long if you keep complaining, Donal."

Adorable as always in a mint-colored polo shirt and tan slacks, Taavi said, "Things will get better, Donal. You'll be acting in our movie soon." He gave the young man a hang loose sign. "And you get to play me ten years older!"

"Thank you. I'm looking forward to it." Donal blinked back tears. "You are a wonderful family."

Mom smiled. "Where is your family, Donal?"

He shrugged. "I was brought up in an orphanage."

"Well, we consider you part of *our* family," she said.

"I'm honored." Donal choked back tears as he made his way over to the buffet. With Hamish shouting after him, Donal brought our plates to the table announcing, "Tonight we have loin of venison with mixed greens, barley, and assorted wild mushrooms."

The second the plate was put in front of Dad, he rammed a piece of venison into his mouth and spilled some sauce onto his Hawaiian shirt. "This is good. I've never eaten a goat before."

Mom laughed. "Venison isn't goat, Dad. It's duck."

I shared a giggle with Noah.

Mom took a picture of her plate for Judy and texted. "Judy said duck is very popular in Viet Nam. So she makes it often for her granddaughter. The little thing comes running into the kitchen for dinner every time Judy calls out, 'Duck Dung!'"

Eating his mushrooms, Dad said, "I'll bet Jack is paying for the duck."

Mom replied, "Tommy and Timmy make a salary."

"How much do they pay nowadays for job hunting?" Dad asked with a smirk.

Donal returned with tea and chocolate cake.

"That reminds me. *Like Water for Chocolate* is on tonight." Dad stuffed a forkful of cake into his mouth.

Martin and Ruben joined us. Donal served them hot cocoa.

"Thank you for remembering, Donal." Martin took a sip. "Mm, it's nice and hot."

"Like the hot water bottle on your feet each night in bed," Ruben replied.

"At least something in bed with me is hot," Martin said with a sniff.

Donal served Martin and Ruben their food and then left us.

Mom prattled on about her day's sightseeing. The she pulled up her next day's destination on her iPhone. "Taavi, since you finished your scenes in the movie, you can come sightseeing with me tomorrow."

"Thank you, Grandma." Taavi looked up at me like a waif in a storm, sighing dramatically and hanging over the back of his chair. "What I'd really like is to help you solve the case, Pop, by acting in a role-play."

"He's part of the family," Martin said, chewing his greens.

Mom was back on her phone. "You'll like this, Taavi. Tomorrow, my bus tour is going to Highland Lookout. It says from there you might spot a Sidhe Fairy!"

"What's a Sidhe Fairy?" Ruben asked between bites of his barley.

Donal was back to clear some plates. "The Sidhe fairies are a separate race of small people who live under the mounds in Scotland and Ireland. If you tell a Sidhe a secret, you will get your wish."

"Aren't the Sidhe a Gaelic (*pronounced gay-lick*) myth?"

Donal's eyes sparkled like the sun kissing the sea. "That's what most people believe."

"*Most* people?" Martin no doubt pondered the romantic life of a fairy (*pun intended*).

Donal whispered, "I've seen them."

"You have?" Martin and Ruben asked in unison.

Donal nodded.

"What do they look like?" Noah asked.

Donal grinned. "Like dark-skinned children wearing blue and gold."

"Where did you see them?" I asked.

"Near the mountains. When I went walking up there six years ago on my twenty-first birthday."

He probably ran into a group of cub scout tourists at night when he was smashed from drinking ale.

Mom asked, "Did the Sidhe fairies grant your wish?"

Donal's dimples appeared. "I didn't ask for one. But I tell you something. If I saw a fairy now, I'd remember to ask for something."

Especially if the fairy was named Brody.

Donal left our table. Noah began gasping and his eyes turned into flying saucers.

"What is it?" I hoped he didn't eat a nut and was going into anaphylactic shock.

"Nicky, I think it's time our son become a man," Noah said.

I put two plus two fairies together. "Elementary, my dear husband."

Catching on, Taavi added, "Let the chase begin!"

As we were leaving the dining room, Noah asked Donal if he would like a friendly ear and a consoling shoulder to cry on over his relationship (or lack thereof) with Brody. Donal jumped at the chance, and my Watson set their meeting for nine-thirty p.m. in the castle lobby. The fairy dust was thrown.

We said goodnight to Mom, Dad, Martin, and Ruben, and then hurried upstairs to our room. Noah went to work with his makeup case, applying silver glitter to Taavi's face. Then we hurried down the hall to our costumer's room. She supervised Taavi's fitting into a long dark wig and a flowing blue robe with gold tassels.

At nine forty-five, Taavi and I were hidden behind a nook in the nearby mountains. I gasped in awe as the sapphire sky embraced the kelly-green mountains and cobalt sea beneath it. We heard Noah and Donal approaching.

"I'm really sorry about your problems with Brody," Noah said with a compassionate look on his handsome face.

"Me too. But talking about it with you helped. And being able to witness your happy marriage with Nicky gives me hope."

"I'm glad."

Donal smiled. "You're an amazing man, Noah."

And?

"And your husband is a real gem."

I always liked Donal.

Noah swayed from side to side like a dancer on a cruise ship.

Donal asked, "Are you all right?"

"I'm just tired from the long day of shooting. I'd better head back to the castle."

"I'll join you," Donal said.

"No. Please. Stay here where it's so beautiful. I can get back to the castle on my own. See you tomorrow."

Before Donal could object, Noah fled faster than a priest chasing a young male parishioner with a daddy fetish. Donal shrugged his small shoulders, scanned the gorgeous landscape, and took in a deep breath.

I nodded Taavi his cue.

As rehearsed by Noah, Taavi spun out like a top, while I rang a bell—courtesy of our film's prop person.

Upon seeing Taavi materialize, Donal stepped backward in a combination of awe, shock, and fear. "Who are you?"

Taavi replied in a high, piercing voice, "I am Via Ta, a Sidhe fairy."

Donal pinched his own arm. "I must be dreaming."

"You seem very much awake to me," Taavi replied.

"Why are you here?" Donal asked in wonderment.

"I come to serve my fairy queen Titania."

A Midsummer Night's Dream?

"But I'm not a fairy," Donal said.

Debatable.

"I'm a mortal," Donal added.

"Are you a good mortal or a bad mortal?"

Is Taavi doing Glinda, the good witch?

Donal replied, "I try to be good. But it isn't always easy."

"Ho-ho-ho." Taavi sat on a rock. "Have you been a bad boy this year?"

Santa Klaus?

Donal's sweet face turned sour. "I've been far better than some other people in Conall Castle."

Taavi sang a bit of *When You Wish Upon a Star.*

That's Cinderella's Castle!

Donal explained, "I'm referring to Conall Castle." He pointed. "Down there. Past the moors and mist."

Taavi said, "Yes. We fairies fly over that castle and throw fairy dust."

Peter Pan?

"Then you know what's going on in there?" Donal asked.

"They are making a movie."

"Yes."

"Starring that little boy who is a very good actor."
Taavi!

"I appeared to you, so I can help you," Taavi said.

Donal asked, "Why *you*?"

"The fairies drew straws. I was the only one who didn't cheat."

"Why appear to *me*?"

"You need help. And helping is my specialty." Taavi rose and did an interpretive dance summoning the powers of the moon, sky, and stars. When he was through, he turned to Donal and cleared his throat. "The Sidhe fairies like applause after we dance."

Donal applauded.

Cheap shot, Taavi. Get to the questions!

"And the Sidhe fairies like to grant mortals a wish." He giggled more like a demon than a fairy. "If mortals tell us their secrets."

"I don't have any secrets."

Taavi leapt off the rock and landed in front of Donal. "The stars tell me you have a very big secret…in your heart. And it is weighing you down."

Donal nodded. "That's true. I'm in love with a man named Brody, who won't love me back. But that's no secret to anyone at Conall Castle."

Taavi ran his toes through the grass. "You work with this Brody?"

Donal replied, "Brody works in Housekeeping. I'm a waiter in the restaurant."

"You do not seem very happy about that."

"That's because I'm not."

Taavi beckoned toward the sea. "The waves are pounding against the shore. They feel your pain, and your desires. I feel your pain too."

A political slogan?

Donal rested his head in his hands. "I want to manage a restaurant. That's no secret either." He let out a pathetic laugh. "But the Conalls made sure that will never happen."

Donal's jaw stiffened. "They put me in my place at Conall Castle, which is lower than where you live under the mound."

"How did they do that?"

"I've never told that to anyone."

"If you tell me, you will get your wish for Brody to love you. And one of the guests at the hotel, Martin, will want to hear all about it"

Really, Taavi?

Donal pondered Taavi's offer. He seemed to realize he had nothing to lose and potentially everything to gain. "A few months ago, late one night, Fergus, the past owner of Conall Castle, came home drunk. He let himself into my room with a pass key from the office. And then he entered my bed and put his hand over my mouth."

"Did he hurt you?"

Donal's eyes filled with tears. "Yeah, he hurt me."

Poor Donal!

"Did you tell anyone?"

"I threatened to the next day, but Fergus said he'd fire me if I did. So, I told his fiancé, Hamish, who didn't believe me. Now Hamish, the current owner, hates me too. And I hate him. Just like I hated Fergus. So, I guess I'm a bad mortal after all." Donal added, "If you can make Brody love someone like me, you're a finer fairy than I am." He walked away.

When Donal was a speck in the distance, Noah came out of hiding behind a nearby tree. Noah, Taavi, and I quietly snuck back to the castle, ran softly up the stairs, and quickly entered our room. After we each showered and got into our T-shirts and boxers, Noah and I sat on either side of Taavi's bed and placed the satin sheet over him.

Broaching the subject carefully, I said, "Taavi, Donal told you something very personal tonight. That means you shouldn't mention it to anyone."

"I know." Taavi replied, "Especially Martin."

Noah and I shared a smile.

"Do you understand why Donal is upset at Fergus and Hamish?" Noah asked.

Taavi nodded. "Sometimes people do mean things to other people. I think Fergus was pretty mean to Donal."

"I think he was too," I said.

Noah added, "And nobody should ever force someone to do something he or she doesn't want to do. Do you understand?"

Taavi nodded again.

"Good." Noah pulled the sheet up to Taavi's chin. "Get some sleep and we'll talk more about this tomorrow."

"Okay."

I kissed Taavi's forehead. "You understand we do these role-plays to try to catch murderers?"

Taavi nodded. "And to play different characters." He grinned.

"Did you have a good time tonight?" Noah asked.

"The best," Taavi said. Fishing for a compliment, he added, "How did I do?"

"You did a great job, son."

"Thanks, Pop."

Noah embraced Taavi. "I was so proud of you."

Taavi hugged him back. "Just like I'm always proud of you and Pop."

When Noah and I were nearly out of the room, Taavi said, "Pop? Dad?"

We stopped at the doorway.

"Tonight, I found something even more fun than being an actor."

"What's that?" Noah and I said in unison.

"Being a detective, like my dads!"

We each blew him a kiss and headed to our room.

Noah and I dove under the sheets of our bed and squeezed each other close.

"I hope we didn't make a mistake letting Taavi do a

role-play. He may be growing up too quickly." I rested my cheek on Noah's smooth neck.

Noah replied, "Taavi's learning the importance of caring for others, and about keeping proper boundaries. A kid can't understand that too soon."

"I agree."

Noah shuddered. "How horrible about Fergus forcing himself on Donal."

"No wonder Donal hated Fergus."

"Donal said he never told anyone about what Fergus did to him. I wonder why he didn't confide in Brody."

"Maybe Donal wanted to take care of Fergus himself."

Noah cocked his head. "Do you think Donal hated Fergus enough to kill him?"

I ran a hand through Noah's thick curls and smelled strawberries. "It wouldn't be the first time a victim felt helpless and took revenge on his attacker."

"Good point."

He sighed. "Why do people hurt other people?"

"That, my dear Watson, is a true mystery." I kissed his soft cheek. "Fergus was a troubled man." I filled Noah in on my visit with Ewan Baird.

My sensitive husband wiped a tear from his cheek. "How horrible for a son not to accept his own father, and for a father not to be able to love his son."

"Agreed."

I lay back and Noah rested his head on my chest. "Nicky, I'm so glad I met you."

"You'll always be the love of my life." I reached down to kiss Noah and received a light snore instead. Resting my head on the soft, thick pillow, I decided to ponder the suspects in the murders. However, sleep, rather than suspects, overtook me.

I woke to an empty bed two hours later. Feeling pangs of déjà vu, I got out of bed, put on my robe and slippers, and headed into the hallway. When I arrived at Brody's door, I heard voices. So, I again ducked behind the wooden column. A few minutes later, Noah exited Brody's room in his robe and slippers. As before, Brody stood in the doorway in his T-shirt and boxers.

Brody scratched at his thick neck, and his shoulders and biceps expanded like melons. "What do you think about the love letters?"

Noah smiled. "I think they're beautiful."

"What do you think they mean?"

"They're *your* letters. You tell me."

Brody tugged at his red beard. "I think it's pretty obvious."

"What are you feeling, Brody?"

"I'm feeling like I don't hate you anymore."

"I'm feeling like I don't hate you anymore either."

Brody's pectoral muscles expanded under his T-shirt. "Are you going to tell Nicky?"

Noah shook his head. "Not yet. I want to be completely sure before I change all of our lives."

Brody nodded. "Then let's meet again privately and see where this goes."

"I'd like that."

Brody smiled. "I think I'd like that too."

Noah hugged Brody and Brody returned the hug.

I raced back to our room, opened the door, and dove into bed. Minutes later, Noah returned and joined me. As I pretended to sleep, I heard him softly whimpering.

Chapter Eight

I woke early the next morning, showered and dressed, and then sat in the tall, wide leather and metal (not what you're thinking) chair opposite our bed. Noah awoke to my questioning stare.

"Nicky." He yawned, rubbed his eyes, and scratched at his hair. "Why are you looking at me like I'm a suspect in the castle murders?"

I slid to the edge of the chair (and got leather burn). "What's going on between you and Brody Naughton?"

He swallowed hard. "What did you overhear last night?"

"We taught Taavi not to answer a question with a question. So how about you answer mine?"

He sat up and rubbed his forehead. "I can't talk about this right now, Nicky."

"Why not?"

"Because I don't fully understand it myself."

"What don't you understand? How you changed from hating Brody to desiring him as a lover?"

Noah burst out laughing. "Nicky, that is so sweet!"

I felt like I was living in an alternate universe.

"After all our years together, you're still jealous!"

I rose and sat at the edge of the bed. "Noah, you're my husband. The love of my life. Of course I'm jealous of you in the arms of another man talking about his love letters in the middle of the night!"

Noah giggled.

"Why won't you tell me what's going on between you and Brody!"

He squeezed my hand. "Nicky, trust me. Brody and I have something to figure out. But it's not what you think. Please, just give me a little more time. Once I have all the answers, I'll explain everything." Noah nibbled on my neck. "Can you do that, Nicky?"

"I guess I have no choice."

"Good." His nibbling continued to my ear and mouth. Then he lay me on my back and took off my blazer. "Now let's get these clothes off."

"I just got dressed."

He took off my shirt. "You don't look dressed to me."

In seconds, our clothes were on the floor. While Noah and I enjoyed some love in the a.m., I couldn't help wondering if he'd rather be with Brody.

After a breakfast of Weetabix and granola cereals with fruit at our table in the Great Hall buffet, I wished Mom a good day sightseeing and Dad an enjoyable time watching television in his room. I also gave Taavi permission to play with Lairie in the dungeon. Then I met up with Martin (in a marigold bowtie and sweater vest), Ruben (in a matching leisure suit), and Noah and Donal (in full kilt costume) in the castle entryway. Noah had used his expert makeup skills to age himself ten years. He had also dyed Donal's hair black and used a tan base on Donal's face. To my surprise, Donal resembled Taavi a great deal, making him the perfect choice to play Older Roddy.

The five of us headed outside to the stone bridge. While Martin and Ruben conversed with the crew, I welcomed Hamish (Prince Jock) and Brody--grrrr (Prince Bruce) in their tunics, kilts, sporrans, long hose, high-laced leather brogues, and cloak drapes. It was no secret that Hamish, Brody, and Donal had never acted before. They scratched at their costumes, winced when our makeup artist applied their touchup makeup, and stood as stiff as a conservative politician meeting a minority constituent in the ninety-nine percent.

In an effort to calm them down, I stood in front of them and painted a broad smile on my face. "Thank you for being in our movie, gents." I rested a hand on Hamish's shoulder and his cloak fell to the stone floor. After resetting it, I said, "Especially you, Hamish. I know this is a very rough time for you."

His button nose crinkled. "As the new laird of Conall Castle, I want to participate. And to follow in the steps of the three lairds before me."

Gee, don't be so broken up about losing your fiancé.

A crocodile peeked out from the moat below and seemed to nod his agreement with me.

"Don't be nervous, everyone. Just listen to your director." I patted my chest. "That's me. Do everything I say, and it will all be over before you know it." *Like a digital rectal exam.*

Moving near me, Noah added, "What Nicky means is that acting is fun. Think back to when you were a child playing pretend. Did you ever play prince or king?"

"I played the princess," Donal said.

"I played the disturbed cousin locked away in the tower," Hamish said.

Martin was at my side. "I played the evil queen."

"Played?" Ruben appeared at my other side.

Undaunted, Noah said, "Imagine you really *are* your character in the movie. Think about how you would act and react to what is going on around you if were him."

Did Noah and Brody just share a smile?

Donal gazed at Brody. "I'm not the new laird of the manor, but I don't have to imagine what it would be like falling in love with Brody, even if he weren't a prince."

Brody melted and rested a strong arm around Donal's small shoulders. "I'm certainly no prince, but I won't have any problem being partnered with you."

"Awwwww!" Martin and Ruben wept and applauded.

Brody instantly released Donal and slapped Donal on the back. "It's all make-believe. So, let's make believe, Donal."

Tears filled Donal's true-blue eyes.

Noah pulled Brody near the ledge of the bridge and they whispered back and forth.

Sweet nothings in each other's ears?

Then Brody walked over to Donal. "I'm sorry."

"You didn't do anything," Donal replied.

"That's the point. And you keep letting me get away with it." Brody ran a hand through his blond beard. "You're a wonderful person. I know that better than anyone. You need to stick up for yourself, Donal."

Standing nearby, Hamish raised his brown eyes to the azure sky. "Poor Donal, always the victim."

Donal seemed ready to give the alligators an early lunch. "Nobody was talking to you, Hamish."

Hamish stomped over to Donal and glared down at him. "And nobody was messing with you that night either."

Brody asked, "What night?"

"It doesn't matter," Donal said.

Hamish chuckled. "That's because it never happened."

"*What* never happened?" Brody asked.

Hamish replied, "My lazy little waiter fabricated a tall tale that Fergus burst into his room one night and took advantage of him. Donal must have fantasized about Fergus so many times, he stopped being able to tell fantasy from reality."

Brody seemed ready to explode. "Is that true, Donal?"

Donal's cheeks reddened. "Fergus was drunk. The next day he told me not to tell anyone." Tears came quickly. "Or I'd lose my job."

"Why didn't you tell me, Donal!"

"It happened a long time ago. It's over, Brody."

Brody sneered at Hamish. "It's a good thing your

boyfriend is dead, or I'd kill him."

Hamish crinkled his button nose. "Fergus may be gone, but I'm not. And don't you both forget I'm laird of Conall Castle now."

Brody grabbed Hamish by the throat. "I don't care if you're laird, king, or god. If you ever touch Donal or push him around, you'll answer to *me*."

"You'll regret that, Brody."

Noah came between Brody and Hamish. "Our goal is to make a movie, not a war."

Brody said to Donal, "We'll talk about this later."

Noah gave the cast acting notes about their individual action, motivation, and intention. Then we rehearsed the epilogue scene in the film. Flashing forward ten years, Donal (older Roddy) and Noah (his mentor Oliver) stood in front of the castle welcoming two new visitors.

Brody said, "Hullo! I am Prince Bruce. This is my brother Prince Jock. We hail from the Hebride Islands."

Martin whispered to me, "Brilliant dialogue!"

"But my brother and I are village people more interested in grooms than brides," Hamish added.

Village people?

"Our stallions are tied up on the cliff. Are we two untied stallions welcome here with ye for a wee respite, lads?" Hamish asked with a wink.

Martin wept, whispering, "This is better than any public television costume drama!"

Donal said, "Aye. I am Roddy, the laird and master of Conall Castle. This is my mentor and friend, Oliver." He gazed into Brody's eyes. "Ye and yer stallion are most welcome here, Prince Bruce."

Brody placed a hand on Donal's shoulder. "I will be a fine guest and do everything ye say, Master Donal."

Noah smiled at Hamish. "And ye have my full support, Prince Jock."

"I look forward to ye teaching me new things, Mentor

Oliver." Hamish winked at Noah.

Ruben whispered to Martin, "Watch many porn films do you, Martin?"

When the rehearsal ended, Noah gave acting notes. After I went over the shots with the DP, we filmed the long shot. Since we were working with first-time actors, a few takes were required before they felt comfortable and were believable in their roles. Then we moved on to the four close-ups. Finally, we broke for a lunch of haddock, potato, and leek stew at the Great Hall's buffet.

As Noah and I sat on wooden stools at the buffet table, I noticed Donal and Brody standing by the large stained-glass window. I (accidentally on purpose) dropped my fork and then kicked it across the stone floor. After retrieving it under a table at the other end of the room, I stayed hidden, watching Donal and Brody.

"Wasn't there anything you could do?" Brody asked.

"Fergus's hand covered my mouth, and his body was so heavy on top of me." Tears slid down Donal's cheeks. "I tried to scream and get free, but I couldn't."

Poor little guy.

Brody looked as if he was going to be sick. "Fergus was worse than Barclay. I'm glad he's with Black Donald now. Why didn't you tell me about this, Donal?"

"I didn't think you would believe me."

"Am I that much of an insensitive brute to you?"

"You're not a brute to me, Brody."

Brody ran a thick hand through his hair. "Noah and Lairie disagree with you."

"That's because they don't know you like I do."

Brody laughed ironically. "Aye, you know my temper." He looked away. "And how I'm afraid to face…who I am."

"Brody, I like who you are. And I want you to like him too." Donal placed his hand over Brody's heart. "Deep inside, the Brody I know is a good man."

They shared a kiss. Then another.

"I don't deserve you," Brody said.

And you don't deserve Noah either!

"But I deserve *you*, Brody." Donal smiled. "A Sidhe Fairy told me so."

Brody laughed. "A Sidhe fairy, aye?"

Donal nodded. "Up on the mountain."

Brody wrapped his arms around Donal. "Did this fairy happen to tell you if I'd wise up and realize you're the best thing that ever happened to me?"

"Something like that."

Good job, Taavi.

They kissed again.

Hamish appeared next to them. Brody pulled away as if Donal were on fire.

"Please, Brody. Don't be afraid." Donal held on to Brody.

Brody glanced from Hamish to Donal and back. After a few moments, he scooped Donal up into his arms and covered his mouth with kisses.

You go, boys.

Hamish rested a hand on his hip. "Donal, now are you going to proclaim that Brody forced himself on you too? I guess you'll say anything to get out of doing your work."

Brody lifted Hamish into the air. "Take that back, Hamish."

"I'll do no such thing!"

"Do it, Hamish!" Brody said.

"Put me down, or you're fired, Brody."

"Don't do this for me, Brody," Donal said at Brody's side.

Brody placed Hamish back onto his feet.

Hamish pulled back his shoulders. "You're fired anyway. Both of you! And your little Lairie too." He rushed off.

Isn't that, "And your little dog too?"

Donal placed his head in his hands. "I'm so sorry,

Brody."

"Don't be. I'm not."

"What are we going to do about work?"

"I'll figure something out," Brody said.

I heard a familiar throat clearing and looked up at Martin and Ruben. "What are you doing on your knees?" Martin asked, clearly excited by the prospects.

Before I could reply, Ruben said, "More importantly, why aren't you calling an end to lunch? We aren't opening a restaurant. We're shooting a movie!"

I adlibbed, "I was just...searching for my contact lens."

"You don't wear contact lenses," Martin answered.

"That's probably why I couldn't find it." I rose and followed Martin and Ruben out of the Great Hall.

When we got outside, the van took us again to the outer parameters of the Conall Castle property. For the rest of the afternoon, we shot a montage of scenes on the emerald-green mountain where Noah (Oliver) and Hamish (Prince Jock) enjoyed spending time together riding horseback and engaging in archery. All went well, except for Noah's horse suddenly lying down on the cliff, causing his trainer to literally "beat a dead horse." A replacement horse was brought in quickly. The expression, "hung like a horse," certainly was true with the understudy horse. I had a hard time keeping the cast focused on each other. However, we finally finished the scene. There was also the little mishap where Noah's arrow (set by Martin) "accidentally" hit Ruben's waving watch. We saved it for the blooper reel.

We moved on to the lake for the nude scene. *That caught your attention.* Noah lay seductively on the large rock with a towel draped over his private area. Hamish exited the lake buck naked, dripping water onto the grass. His tall, muscular body glowed like a Scottish gods' in the golden afternoon sunlight. Fortunately, or unfortunately, a large piece of seaweed had wrapped itself around

Hamish's torso, providing the scene with an R rating. *Where's a seaweed-loving sea turtle when you need one?* Even though I kept reminding myself that Noah was playing a character in a film, I felt a pang of jealousy as Noah and Hamish kissed. However, I was thankful that it wasn't Brody that Noah was kissing. At least not in the movie!

Next, we shot Donal (Older Roddy) and Brody (Prince Bruce) walking together on the violet moor. They grew tired and lay on the amber heather. (I couldn't help thinking of the poppy fields in *The Wizard of Oz*.) With the cerulean sky blanketing them, Brody leaned over and planted a sweet kiss on Donal's lips. Donal returned the kiss, and the two men were in each other's arms, hugging, kissing, and looking very much in love. The two men slid out of their clothes, and they made beautiful R-rated love, courtesy of the tall heather. So much for Brody's abandon. He was so into the scene, he could have won a Grabby Award!

When we finished shooting, we all boarded the van. I sat with Martin and Ruben and enjoyed the gorgeous view of the foamy sea reaching out to the ancient lighthouse in the distance.

"That was some hot scene!" Martin waved his palm near his cheek. "When I wrote it, I imagined myself with a 'straight' A-list, rugged, sexy, young movie star."

"'Imagine' is the operative word," Ruben said.

Martin ignored him. "Brody and Donal turned out to be good actors."

"They weren't acting," I replied.

"Do tell." Martin looked like a drug addict in a failed rehab program.

I explained, "I *happened* to overhear Brody and Donal declare their love for each other."

"That must have been when you were on your knees under the Great Hall table spying on them," Ruben added.

Martin shooed away his husband like a poisonous

wasp. "What's wrong with spying? The Russians have done it for years, and it won them the presidential election in the US. Go on, Nicky."

I said, "Brody still seems to be working out some issues of internalized homophobia."

"Like Ruben," Martin said.

Ruben and I did a doubletake.

"When Ruben and I met, he wasn't comfortable being gay," Martin said.

"That's because you insisted on making love with the lights on." Ruben glanced over at me. "Believe me, Nicky. Even then Martin wasn't a pretty sight."

"Oh, you were crazy about me." Martin slapped his husband's shoulder. "And you still are."

"Crazy is the word."

They smooched.

Mid-kiss, Martin asked me, "What about 'the widow' Hamish?"

"He doesn't seem too broken up about Fergus's death," Ruben said.

"Especially since Hamish is now laird of the castle and can fire whomever he chooses," I said.

"Who did Hamish fire?" Martin asked, at the edge of his seat.

"Brody, Donal, and Lairie," I replied.

"The plot thickens," Martin said.

Ruben stared at his watch. "And time ticks away. We need to shoot the last scene!"

Once back at the castle, our crew set up in one of the sitting rooms. Noah gave the other three actors acting notes. I conferred with the DP, and Ruben growled at the antique clock on the oak table.

I called for quiet. Since it was past dinnertime, and the scene was a short one, we skipped the rehearsal and shot the long shot. Donal (Older Roddy) and Brody (Prince Bruce) lay on a leather chaise in a windowed turret with a stunning view of the moors in the distance. On a burgundy sofa, next to the tall stone fireplace, lay Noah (Oliver) and Hamish (Prince Jock). The two couples kissed. (Grrrr.) Donal glanced across the room at Noah and said, "A man's home is his castle."

Noah winked at him. "Ye learned well."

I called, "Cut!"

Behind the camera operator, tears ran down Martin's cheeks. "The script is a masterpiece! I'm going to write my Oscar acceptance speech tonight!"

"Be sure to keep the speech under a minute." Ruben smirked. "Actually, a pipe dream can be as long as you like." Then he rolled his hand in the air and pointed to an antique clock on an end table.

We repeated the scene with a close-up on each couple. The second we were through, Ruben shouted, "It's a wrap!"

Everyone cheered.

Noah was at my side. "You did it again, Mr. Director."

"Yes, I did!" I kissed his cheek.

"Didn't somebody help you?" Noah asked.

"Of course. Martin's script was camp heaven, and Ruben kept me directing at breakneck speed."

"Nicky, aren't you forgetting someone?"

I slapped my forehead. "How could I forget Taavi. He was such a little professional on this shoot."

"And?"

"And all the deceased actors will be remembered fondly." *As soon as I figure out who killed them.*

Brody joined us. "Thanks, guys. I enjoyed this." He rested a hand on Noah's shoulder. "You helped me a lot, Noah. I appreciate that."

"Thank you, Brody. I'm glad *somebody* noticed me." Noah stomped out of the room.

"What's with Noah?" I asked myself aloud.

Brody replied, "Even an insensitive brute like me can

see Noah just wants a little credit for his good work."

"Right. I knew that." *The Insensitive Husband Award goes to Nicky the creep Abbondanza.* I caught up to Noah at the lip of the grand staircase in the hallway. I said like a puppy with his tail between his legs, "It's not a good excuse, but the truth is I didn't thank you because we're a team." I kissed his tight lips. "Nicky and Noah. Soulmates for life." I sighed. "And also because I'm a self-centered egomaniac."

Noah's face softened. "But you're *my* self-centered egomaniac." He kissed my sideburn. "And it takes one egomaniac to know another."

I took him in my arms. "What did *this* egomaniac ever do to deserve you?"

"You solved the theatre department murders case at Treemeadow." He pinched my ab. "With my help." He squeezed my nipple. "And you took all the credit."

We shared a long kiss.

"I could never do a play or movie or solve a murder mystery without you." I rested my cheek against his. "Or live happily ever after."

"I couldn't live without you, Nicky."

"And you never will."

We walked arm in arm to the Great Hall, where we were welcomed and seated at our family table by a waiter we hadn't seen before.

Martin whispered to me, "Looks like you were right about Hamish firing Donal."

"Poor sweet little, Donal. He was a wonderful waiter." Mom waved her iPhone. "Judy wants to know why he was let go."

"Because Hamish, like his deceased fiancé, was a bully," I replied.

Lairie appeared in front of us in a long black dress. "Nicky, I want to thank you for starring me in your movie."

Starring you?

"And to say goodbye." She clasped her hands to her chest and swayed from side to side. "My father and I will soon be destitute."

Brody, having changed into jeans and a steel-blue shirt that matched his eyes, stood next to his daughter. "Let the people eat in peace, Lairie."

"But we're going to be homeless! Why can't we go to the States with Nicky, Noah, and Taavi?" She cried into her father's chest.

Taavi's face turned the color of his cherry dress shirt. "My dads will help you and your father, Lairie."

Dad glanced at Noah. "Brody and Lairie were fired too?"

Noah nodded. "Hamish told them earlier today."

Rising, Dad said, "I'm sorry to hear that, Brody."

Brody looked down at his beard. "Thank you."

"Hamish did a terrible thing," Dad added.

"We'll be all right," Brody said.

"After our movie releases, my fans will demand to see more of me." Lairie took my hand. "And you'll have to star me in your next movie."

"We need to edit this film first and see about distribution," I explained.

Noah said, "Brody, you have my number if you need anything."

Grrrrrr.

"Aye." Brody pulled Lairie away. "We need to get back upstairs and finish packing. Donal will have my head for leaving him to do all of it." They left.

Our waiter served us mince, tatties, kedgeree, crowdie, and honeycomb toffee with tea. Translated into Americanese, that's beef and carrots; potato; a casserole of fish, rice, egg, and curry; cream cheese; and honeycomb toffee with tea.

Dad sat back down and dove into the mince. "Mm, it tastes just like my favorite dish: meatloaf."

Not exactly a sophisticated palate.

As Mom offered us an iPhone slideshow of her day's sightseeing, and Taavi reenacted the fun he'd had playing in the dungeon with Lairie, I wondered why Hamish wasn't in the Great Hall. Surely, the ex-host and current laird of Conall Castle would want to greet his guests at dinner.

I finished eating (and swallowing my vitamins and milk thistle capsules) and led my group up the long staircase to our rooms. After we said goodnight to Mom and Dad and Martin and Ruben in the hallway, Noah and I tucked in Taavi. Then we headed for our room next door, stripped to our T-shirts and boxers, hopped into our canopied bed, and hugged and kissed under the white satin sheet.

"Where do you think Hamish was tonight?" I asked.

As we lay on our backs, Noah nestled his head in the fold of my neck and the scent of strawberries filled the bed. "Maybe he was…doing whatever the laird of the castle does."

"Hm."

Noah slid onto his side. "Do you think Hamish is our murderer, and he was off planning how to kill his next victim?"

"Killing the three Conall brothers to inherit this place is definitely a strong motive."

"But why kill Moira?"

"Perhaps Moira knew what Hamish was up to." As we fell asleep in each other's arms, I thought about the missing piece of the puzzle.

I woke up an hour later to an empty bed. *Really, Noah?*

In what was becoming my nightly routine, I put on my robe and slippers, checked on Taavi sleeping peacefully, headed down the hallway, and waited behind the wooden column for Noah to leave Brody's room.

The door opened, and Noah exited in his robe and

slippers, holding a letter. "This is so beautiful," Noah said with tears in his eyes. "Thank you for giving it to me."

Brody (wearing only his boxers!) ran a hand through his thick blond hair. "It's heartfelt."

"Of course."

"Your father said it's okay."

Did he ask Dad for Noah's hand in marriage? Noah is already married. To me!

Brody asked, "Do you know what this means?"

Noah nodded, and the two men embraced.

Grrrrrr.

Brody said, "I'm ready to tell Lairie and Donal about us."

"I want to tell Nicky."

It's about time!

Brody rested a hand on Noah's shoulder. "Are you really okay with this?"

Noah nodded. "At first I wasn't. But now, I'm *very* okay with this."

"Aye, me too."

They shared a smile.

"Come back inside."

"Don't you want some time to sort this out?"

"I want you beside me."

"It's my pleasure." Noah followed Brody, and the door shut.

Having had enough of this charade, with my heart pounding like a bass drum, I hurried to Brody's door and banged on it. A moment later, Brody answered, and I pushed past him, ready to have it out with Noah once and for all. To my surprise, I found Noah and Dad sitting on the sofa with a pile of old letters and a half four-leaf clover necklace between them.

"Nicky! What are you doing here?" Noah asked.

As if watching flashbacks in a movie, I recalled snippets of events over the week: Dad wearing the two-leaf clover necklace he had gotten in Scotland before he had met Mom, Dad's surprise at dinner when he heard the name of Brody's mother, Dad asking Noah and Brody to stop arguing at dinner, Dad calling Noah upstairs when Noah and Brody battled in the hallway, Dad's role-play question about Elsbeth's looks, Dad defending Brody to Mom at dinner, Dad's offer to help Brody and Lairie when he heard Hamish had fired them, and Ewan's comment about Elsbeth's "secret." I collapsed into an easy chair. "Noah and Brody are brothers!"

Dad blinked back tears. "It seems that way."

Noah explained, "Dad had a suspicion after meeting Brody. I told Brody about it, and he dug up his mother's old letters signed, 'Love, Scott.' He also found her necklace, just like Dad's. And a letter she wrote, but never mailed."

"The letter was written to me." Dad wiped a tear off his cheek.

"Everything was hidden in the back of my mother's vanity drawer. I found them a year ago after my parents passed, but I never read them." Brody smiled at Noah. "Until now."

"The letters chronicle Elsbeth's relationship with Dad while he was in Scotland as a young man." Noah grinned at his father. "Dad was quite a romantic back then."

"In my last letter, I told Elsbeth that I had met Bonnie," Dad said. "And that I wouldn't write back again."

Brody added, "Mom wrote that she was expecting Scott's child. But she never mailed the letter for fear of ruining Scott's marriage to Bonnie. Soon afterward, she met my father. They were married a month later, and he claimed me as his own."

I sounded like a strangled frog. "Noah, why didn't you tell me?"

He rose and sat on the arm of my chair. "I wanted to, but I had to be sure before announcing that I have a brother. So Brody and I found the letters and read each one."

"I didn't need any letters." Dad smiled at Brody. "I knew Brody was my son."

"How do you feel about that?" Brody asked him.

"I feel fine. Just fine." With tears streaming down his chubby cheeks onto his T-shirt, Dad stood and opened his arms.

Brody came to him and they shared a long embrace. When they parted, Brody said, "When my parents died a year ago in that plane crash, a tough shell grew around me. I never thought I'd have another chance to have a father."

"Well, you've got one now," Dad said. "And I want us to have a relationship. I mean, if that's what you want."

"I'd like that too." Brody grimaced. "But I'm not so sure Noah feels the same way as you do about his half-brother—the arrogant closet case."

Noah stood face to face with Brody. "You're right. I don't feel the same way as my dad." He grinned like a schoolboy with a worm-infested apple for his teacher. "*I'm* excited about having an older brother to buy me gifts, listen to my problems—"

"And to keep you in your place," Brody said.

They shared a smile.

Brody said, "Noah, I know I've acted like a fool. And I understand we're strangers living in two different countries. But I'd like to get to know my half-brother."

"I'd like you in my life too," Noah said. "And as your half-brother, it's my place to say something else."

"What?" Brody asked.

"You're a total idiot."

"Why?" Brody said with raised shoulders.

"For not thanking your lucky Scottish stars for Donal," Noah said. "Donal is a wonderful man. And for some unknown reason, he is madly in love with you. Don't mess that up, brother."

Brody laughed. "I don't intend to."

"Good."

Brody offered a strong hand. Noah hugged him. Then he pointed at me. "Of course, my husband, the detective, figured it all out."

"I sure did." I cringed. "After I thought you two were lovers."

Noah screeched, "My own brother!"

"That's pretty kinky," Brody said. "Even for an American."

We all shared a laugh.

Noah asked, "You didn't really think there was anything going on between Brody and me?"

"Not really." I waited for my nose to grow.

Something else grew when Noah sat on my lap and put his arms around me. "You're the only man for me, Nicky Abbondanza."

With my pulse rate down to about a hundred and fifty, I thanked the Scottish gods that my fears were unfounded. Mid-kiss, we heard a crash coming from downstairs. "Noah, look in on Taavi."

Dad got to the door first. "I'll make sure Mom is okay."

"I'll check on Lairie and Donal," Brody said.

I ran out of the room. Taking the steps two at a time, I reached the downstairs hallway. The knight's armor lay on the stone floor. I knelt at its side and removed the helmet. A familiar sweet smell laced the air as Hamish's lifeless face stared up at me. *Good (k)night, Hamish.*

CHAPTER NINE

Later that night, I sat on a long leather sofa in a castle sitting room off the hallway. Since it was a cool early-summer night, flames of amber, tangerine, and amaranth danced in the wide hearth of the white stone fireplace opposite me. Chief Inspector Lennox Frazier stood in front of me searching in each of his pockets for a notepad and pen. Finally locating the notepad under his left sock, Frazier retrieved it, and then accidentally dropped it into the fireplace. "Butterfingers!"

Inspector Owen Steward lunged toward the fire.

In an effort to save the younger inspector from burning his hands, Frazier reached out to him, thereby poking his fingers in the young man's eyes. "Sorry."

"That's all right, Lennox, I mean, Chief Inspector." Tearing and blinking, Owen got down on all fours like a nearsighted dog and felt his way around the burning embers. When his fingers were dustier than a crematory operator's, he said, "I don't want you to lose your brilliant notes on the case, sir."

"No need, Owen, I mean, Inspector." Frazier pointed to his temple. "Everything is also stored here. Let me help you up." He reached down and clasped hands with Owen. Since Owen was finally able to open his eyes, the two men gazed at each other.

I heard violins. Or maybe it was termites gnawing through the ancient wood molding.

As Frazier assisted Owen to his feet, the Chief

Inspector lost his balance, and the two men toppled over at my feet, knocking over the fireplace poker.

Did Owen wrap his arms around Frazier's stocky back a bit too tightly? And did Frazier remain on top of Owen a tad too long?

After a number of apologies, the two men were on their feet (for the moment). Frazier rested a hand on his hip that slid down to his knee. "I'm glad you called us, Nicky." He searched his pockets." Oh, my notepad is burnt to bits in the fireplace, isn't it?

"I'll remember anything you need to write, sir." Owen offered Frazier a warm smile atop the younger man's bouncing Adam's Apple.

"Thank you, Owen, ah, Inspector." Frazier sat next to me on the sofa. Feeling it about to topple over, I steadied the sofa in the upright position. "Please tell me again what you found, Nicky."

"Hamish MacAlastair was lodged inside the knight's armor in the entryway of the castle."

Frazier nodded. "Death no doubt by suffocation."

"Not exactly." I explained, "I smelled ethylene glycol."

"Ethylene glycol?" Frazier asked.

Owen said, "Antifreeze, sir, which I'm sure you knew."

"Of course. Remember that, Owen, Inspector." Frazier scratched at his wide chest. "At least MacAlastair didn't die from frost bite." He laughed at his own joke.

Owen guffawed wildly.

I steadied the sofa. "My guess is the forensic testing won't show fingerprints, since the murderer was probably wearing gloves."

"But there may be fibers, hair, or some other important clue," Frazier said.

"Very smart, sir," Owen added with a proud nod.

"I learned that from my father," Frazier said with a satisfied sniff.

"Lennox's, rather the Chief Inspector's father was

Chief Superintendent Balloch Frazier," Owen added.

"So I've heard. *Again and again.*

Frazier crossed one leg over the other, leaned his elbow on it, and slid down, banging his nose on his knee. "Sorry."

"It can happen to anyone." Owen stood over him. "The material in the suits nowadays are quite tapered and slippery. Particularly when a man fills his suit so fully."

Is he gaping at Frazier?

"Yes, well." Frazier rubbed his thick neck. "We definitely have a mass murderer here in Conall Castle."

No shit, Sherlock. "It seems pretty clear that someone is killing the owners of Conall Castle."

"I don't follow," Frazier said.

Owen interceded with, "The Chief Inspector understands your theory, Professor. He means that he would like you to elaborate on it—so he can tell you where you are correct and where you are misguided."

I explained, "Kendric and Emilia Conall died in a car accident off a cliff a year ago. This week, Barclay, Magnus, Moira, and Fergus Conall were all murdered here on the castle grounds or at the castle itself."

"But Moira Conall never inherited Conall Castle," Owen said.

"True, but the murderer might not have known that," I replied.

"How does Hamish MacAlastair fit into this?" Frazier asked.

Owen replied, "The Chief Inspector is testing you, Professor. He knows Hamish was engaged to Fergus Conall, and that thanks to Fergus's will, Hamish inherited Conall Castle."

"Is that right?" After a glance from Owen, Frazier said, "That's right. Of course."

I rose and paced the room in Sherlock Holmes mode. "So, the question is who owns Conall Castle now?"

"Damned if I know. There aren't any Conall's left!"

Frazier said.

Owen raised his hand as if one of my students.

"Owen?" I said with a nod.

"I took the liberty of making a few calls, and I found out that Hamish's will leaves everything he had to Fergus."

"Isn't Fergus deceased too?" Frazier asked.

"As you well know, sir," Owen responded.

Frazier sighed. "If my parents were alive, they could help me figure this out."

Owen explained, "Lennox's, rather the Chief Inspector's parents were the Chief Superintendent and Conall Castle bookkeeper respectively. That is before Lennox's, I mean, the Chief Inspector's father died of a heart attack a few years back, and his mother passed from cancer last year. Terrible tragedies both."

Frazier smiled at Owen. "Thank you for saying that, Owen."

Owen blushed. "They were your parents after all, Lennox, I mean Chief Inspector." He covered his mouth with his long, thin hand. "But that's not to say, Professor, that Chief Inspector Frazier can't solve the case without their help. I'd bet all my money on him!"

And your heart. I remembered something Ewan had told me in the abbey. It suddenly hit me quicker than a conservative politician taking away his constituents' medical insurance. "I think I know who is next in line to inherit Conall Castle!"

"Who?" Frazier and Owen said in unison.

They do it too! As I hurried out of the room, I shouted over my shoulder, "I need to speak with someone before I can tell you."

I ran upstairs and entered our room. With Noah in bed, I told him my plan. Then I slipped a note under Brody and Lairie's, Donal's, and Mom and Dad's rooms, requesting a meeting in our room first thing in the morning. As I drifted off to sleep with Noah snoring softly on my chest, I wondered if my theory was right.

The next morning, after room service breakfast of porridge with a touch of whiskey, orange juice, and vitamins and milk thistle capsules for me, Noah and I stood at the tall stone fireplace in our room. Opposite us on the leather sofa sat Mom and Dad. Taavi and Lairie dangled their legs over the edge of the vast canopy bed. Brody and Donal sat on the turreted burgundy window seat in front of the long velvet burgundy drapes.

I nodded to Noah. He took a deep breath and said, "Mom, Lairie, the men met up last night in Brody's room. We discovered something pretty shocking." He smiled at Brody. "But also pretty terrific."

Mom grasped her iPhone on the lap of her turquoise dress, placing her fingers in texting mode. "What is it?"

Dad took her hand. "I told you that I came to northern Scotland before I met you."

"Of course," Mom said.

"But I didn't tell you that while I was here, I fell in love…with a woman named Elsbeth."

The makeup cracked on Mom's forehead. "Why does that name sound familiar?"

Brody cleared his throat. "Elsbeth was my mother. She worked here at the castle in Housekeeping." He blinked back a tear. "She died a year ago in a plane crash."

Dad lifted the two-leaf clover necklace from underneath his Hawaiian shirt. "Elsbeth gave me this. I gave her the other half."

Brody lifted the hem of his gray sweatshirt and took the identical necklace from his jeans' pocket. "This was my mother's. She put it on this chain and kept it in the back of a drawer inside her vanity."

"Elsbeth and I wrote letters back and forth." Dad

squeezed Mom's hand. "Until I met you, and I realized you were the one."

Noah said, "But what Dad didn't know was that Elsbeth also fell in love and married Robbie Naughton, the castle caretaker."

Mom smiled. "I like stories with happy endings."

"But that wasn't the end." Dad fidgeted in his seat. "Elsbeth had a child." He swallowed hard. "My child."

Mom dropped her iPhone onto the sofa.

Dad took her hands. "But Elsbeth didn't tell me. All these years she raised the boy with Robbie as his father, because she didn't want to break up our marriage, and theirs."

"How do you know this?" Mom asked with a dry throat.

Brody explained, "I found my mother's old letter…to Scott. She never mailed it."

Mom gasped. "Brody is your son?"

Dad nodded.

Running a quivering hand through his beard, Brody added, "It was a shock to me too."

"Are you sure about this?" Mom asked.

Noah answered, "Brody and I investigated it. I believe Brody is my half-brother."

"How do you feel about that, Noah?" Mom asked with her mouth still agape.

Noah moved next to his mother and rested a hand on her shoulder. "I was surprised and leery at first. But I'm feeling good about it now, Mom."

Brody rose and walked over to Mom. "I know this is sudden, and crazy, after all these years. But I wasn't very close to my dad. And I was an only child. If it's not too late, I'd like to have a relationship with my father and half-brother. But don't worry about me coming between you and your husband, or you and your son. That won't happen." He scratched at his blond hair. "I hope you don't hate me for dredging all this up thirty-seven years later. The last thing I want to do is cause trouble."

Mom stared out the window in thought. Then she stood and turned to Brody. "Dad and I were so excited when Noah was born. He was always the perfect son. And he still is."

Noah's cheeks turned pink.

"We wanted more children." Mom's face sagged. "But that never happened." She took Brody's hand in hers. "Until now." Sitting Brody down between her and Dad she said, "I won't pretend this isn't a shock." She glared at Dad. "And I will certainly have a few words with my husband for not telling me about this sooner. But I couldn't be happier to have another son, especially a son who I've realized is a good, honest man. A son like you." She embraced Brody and he wept on her shoulder. Then she took Brody's face in her hands. "And my first act as your stepmother is to call you a fool if you don't ask that sweet, adorable, wonderful young man over there to marry you."

"I was just about to do that very thing." Brody got to his feet, rushed over to Donal, and knelt beside him. "Donal, I've been more foolish than all of the Conalls put together. I finally admit my love for you. And the minute we get outside, I'm going to shout it proudly and merrily from the cliffs, mountains, and moors. I won't blame you if you're through with me. But since you have a loving and forgiving heart, I hope you will give me another chance by marrying me and being part of my family with Lairie."

Donal jumped up, raised Brody to his feet, and threw his arms around him. After they shared a long embrace, Donal blew a kiss to Mom.

On the sofa, Mom blew back the kiss, and then rested her head on Dad's shoulder. He placed his arm around her and whispered in her ear of his love for her.

"Well?" Brody wiped the perspiration off his forehead. "What's your answer?"

Donal laughed. "My answer is 'yes!'"

Brody and Donal kissed, and then reached out their arms to Lairie. She joined them for a warm family hug.

Taking center stage, or rather standing in the center of the room, I said, "Brody, though she never mailed it, your mother was honest in her last letter to Dad about his paternity. Don't you think this would be a good time for you to be honest with Lairie about *her* father?"

Brody asked me, "How did you know?"

"I visited Ewan Baird in the old abbey," I replied.

"Who's Ewan Baird?" Mom asked.

"Your leprechaun," I said. "He was caretaker of the abbey many years ago, and he remained there as a fixture." Feeling like the host of a television reality show, I said, "Ewan mentioned the waitress Fenella and Magnus Conall were once lovers. Due to class differences and pressure from Magnus's father Kendric, Fenella and Magnus didn't marry. After some prodding from Brody's father Robbie, Brody and Fenella married instead. But shortly after giving birth to Lairie, Fenella ran off with Balfour, the bartender." I walked over and rested a hand on Brody's shoulder. "I'm guessing you raised Fenella and Magnus's child as your own."

Brody replied, "When Fenella and Balfour ran off and left Lairie with me, I told Lairie I was her dad, which was fine with Magnus." His face softened. "I don't regret it. I love this girl as if she were my own." He wiped a tear from his nose. "And she is."

"You're a good man, Brody." Dad beamed like a meteor. "And you come from good stock." He headed over and embraced his son.

Brody placed a strong arm around the girl. "Lairie, I made so many mistakes in my life. But the one thing I did right was raise you. I loved you more than life itself. You meant everything to me, and you still do. You are my daughter. And you always will be."

Donal rested his hand on her other side. "I've never seen a man love a daughter as much as your father has always loved you, Lairie." He kissed her cheek. "Are you terribly shocked, honey?"

"I'm not shocked at all." Lairie took her father's hand. "I heard you and Magnus talking about it when I was five years old."

"Why didn't you ever say anything!" Brody asked.

"Magnus was ashamed of me. Fenella ran away from me. The Conalls wouldn't bury your parents in their cemetery. I had no interest in being a member of such a hateful, horrible family. And I'm glad they're all gone."

"I'm lost," Dad said. "Is this like in *Kramer vs. Kramer*?"

Mom explained, "Magnus Conall and Fenella were Lairie's birth parents, but Brody is the father of her heart because he raised the girl as his own."

Seeming to have aged ten years, Lairie looked majestic in her white dress. "I don't care who brought me into the world. My dad and Donal are my family." She threw herself into their arms, and the three of them wept together. After a few moments, Lairie broke free and said to Dad, "And I hope you'll allow me to be part of my father's new family."

"We would have it no other way." Dad joined their group hug.

Mom was next. "I always wanted a granddaughter! Like Judy has Dung!"

"And I'm excited to have a niece!" Noah joined the huddle.

Taavi entered last. "And now I have another uncle and cousin!"

"How cool!" Lairie said.

With everyone hugging and crying, I let out a sharp whistle. "I hate to break up the family reunion, but there's another really important matter to discuss." When I had everyone's attention, I said, "Since Lairie is the only living

Conall, she inherits Conall Castle."

Lairie jumped up and down in fits of joy. "I'm really mistress of Conall Castle, Taavi! I don't have to pretend any longer!"

"You'll be a terrific owner, Lairie!" Taavi said.

Lairie rubbed her hands together. "And I won't be a vicious boss like Barclay, Magnus, Fergus, and Hamish!"

"Can I be your knight?" Taavi asked.

"Of course!" she replied.

I whistled again. "More importantly, someone has been murdering the past owners of Conall Castle. I don't want to scare anyone, but Lairie may be the murderer's next target!"

"Then you'd better figure out the murderer's identity soon, Nicky." Mom retrieved her iPhone from the sofa. "I have a lot of catching up to do with Judy. She may have Dung on her lap, but I'll have Lairie!"

Dad hugged Brody, Donal, and Lairie to his chest. "Come on, I want to become acquainted with my son, his intended, and my granddaughter—the mistress of Conall Castle." As they all left our room, Dad said to me over his shoulder, "We did the hard part—acting in the role-plays. Now figure out who did it, Nicky."

I called out, "Watch over Lairie. Don't let her out of your sight for a minute!"

"We won't," Brody and Donal said.

They do it too!

I pulled Noah and Taavi back into our room and shut the door. After sitting Taavi back on the bed, I stood over him with my hand on his shoulder. "Do you understand everything that went on here this morning?"

He nodded, looking grown up in a banana-colored polo shirt and jeans.

Noah sat next to him and rested his arm around the boy. "Do you have any questions for us?"

Taavi nodded again. "When can Brody and Lairie

come visit us in Vermont?"

"Soon. But we want to know if you understand…"

Since Noah wasn't getting anywhere, I chimed in with, "Do you have any questions about…the process of how…"

Taavi grinned from ear to ear. "Pop, Dad, before we met in Hawaii, I knew about how babies were made. It's a pretty simple thing to understand." He placed a hand on each of our shoulders. "But after you adopted me, I learned something even cooler. And I learned it again just now. A kid's real parents are the people who love him and take care of him." He gave us the hang loose sign.

The three of us shared a long hug.

Then Taavi reached inside the night table and handed me my laptop. "It's time for you to make your list, Pop."

"We know you can do it, Nicky," Noah said with a wink. Then he lifted Taavi from the bed. "Come on, let's go make sure Lairie is all right."

"Dad, what should we call Lairie now that she's the mistress of Conall Castle?"

"I think 'Lairie' is just fine," Noah replied. He mouthed, "Good luck," to me, and then led Taavi out of the room.

Sitting on the bed, I phoned Frazier to tell him the latest news. He said he'd send an officer to watch over Lairie. Then I sat cross-legged and placed the laptop in front of me on the bed. Instead of making notes about the murders, I Skyped my brother and looked into the computer at myself—if I were younger. *Grr.* "Hi, Tony."

Tony's biceps bulged out of his white T-shirt as he ran a strong hand through his thick black hair. "Do you know what time it is, bro?"

"Early morning in New York City, but afternoon here in Scotland. How's my brother the Broadway choreographer?"

He yawned. "Tired. And it's your fault."

"What did *I* do?"

"You got me started on the great white dance way." He rubbed his sagging eyelids. "We rehearsed late last night for the new show."

"How come?"

"Our director impregnated our leading lady who had to leave the show on doctor's orders. Her first understudy is the director's wife, who quit in anger. The second understudy is the first understudy's lover, so she quit in solidarity with her girlfriend. Are you following this?"

"Unfortunately, yes."

Tony scratched his Roman nose. "To cut to the chase, I had to rehearse the third understudy, the director's male lover, who is doing the role in drag."

I sighed. "I miss the theatre."

"No you don't. You're a big movie director now."

"Yeah, shooting films in a week on a budget the size of one of Mama's poker chips."

He smiled. "How's Scotland? I've never been there. And, yes, that's a hint."

"Scotland's beautiful. And there are no dance sequences in the movie." I cocked my head. "Come to think of it, a dance or two might have helped."

"Too late. We open here in two days. How are Noah and Taavi?"

"Waiting for a visit from you."

"They always did like me best." Tony giggled.

"How's your spouse?"

"Fine. He's at the church, missing me like crazy." His abs rippled underneath the T-shirt. "Bro, I'm not a farmer. You didn't call me at this ungodly hour to make chitchat. I'm guessing you're having trouble figuring out whodunit."

My jaw dropped. "How do you know people are being murdered at Conall Castle?"

"Because wherever you go, whenever you go there, people are murdered, Nicky. I can't believe anyone does a show with you, let alone travel with you. You're like a tomb filled with zombies. An extermination camp. An outbreak of a rare and untreatable infectious disease."

"All right, Tony, I get it! And yes, I'm having some difficulty figuring this one out."

Tony leaned forward, and his shoulders filled half the screen. "Listen, bro, I have to shower and get back to the theatre. So, I'll make this fast. Think of your investigation like a dance. Take one step at a time. Put one foot in front of the other. Keep in time. Don't miss any moves. Use your mind, body, and spirit. And don't forget a splashy finish."

I grinned. "Thanks, Tony."

"Hey, what are brothers for? Now make your list and figure this thing out."

After we disconnected, my fingers hit the keyboard.

The Conall Castle Murders

Victims: Barclay Conall, Magnus Conall, Moira Conall, Fergus Conall, Hamish MacAlastair

Suspects and Motives:
1) *Brody Naughton: angry that the Conalls refused to bury his parents in the Conall family cemetery; had a bad break-up with Barclay; jealous that Magnus was Lairie's real father; found the Conalls to be unreasonably tough bosses; enraged that Fergus raped Donal; angry that Hamish bullied Donal; mad that Hamish fired Donal, Lairie, and him.*
2) *Lairie Naughton: yearned to be mistress of Donal Castle; knew she was a secret heiress and the Conalls and Hamish stood in her way; resented Magnus for rejecting her as his daughter; blamed Barclay for the messy breakup between Brody and Barclay; believed Barclay, Magnus, Moira, Fergus, and Hamish to be vicious bosses; angry at Hamish for firing the three of them.*
3) *Donal Blair: jealous of Barclay's past relationship with*

Brody; overworked and abused by Fergus and Hamish;
angry that Hamish fired the three of them.

I stared at the computer screen. *It could be any of them.*
What am I missing? I Skyped a familiar address. "Hi, Mama
and Papa."

My parents' kind and full faces filled the computer
screen. Mama clutched at the collar of her black flannel
robe. "Nicky, how is your vacation going?"

"Scotland is a gorgeous country," I said.

"Not as gorgeous as Italy," Mama said.

"Conall Castle is pretty amazing," I replied.

"Not as amazing as the castles in Italy," Papa said.

I sighed.

"Do they have gambling at your castle?" Mama
salivated like a cat at a sardine canning factory.

"No, Mama. No gambling," I said.

"Then why stay there?" she asked.

I replied, "Conall Castle is thousands of years old with
beautiful stone and stained-glass windows."

"The stone and stained-glass windows in Italy are
better," Mama said.

"And the mountains, cliffs, sea, lakes, meadows, and
moors in Scotland are stunning," I replied.

"Not as stunning as in Italy," Papa said.

"There's an old abbey here," I said.

Papa scratched at his bald head and his jowls shook
like gelatin. "I bet it's not as old as St. Peter's Basilica in
Italy."

Mama's dark eyes lit up like shooting stars. "When we
vacationed in Italy, Papa and I saw the Pope! He wore a
beautiful violet dress. And he was surrounded by altar
boys serving him."

I'm sure.

"And secret police were everywhere," Dad added.
"The Catholic Church has its own force you know!"

"But none of them can solve mysteries like my son,"

Mama said with a definitive nod.

Until now.

"And our son's husband." Dad tied the belt of his black robe. "How is our wonderful son-in-law?"

"Noah's fine, Papa."

"Why aren't Noah and Taavi with you?" Mama asked.

"They're with Noah's new brother."

"Bonnie and Scott had a child at their age!" Mama clutched at her heart.

I explained, "No, Brody's older than Noah. He's Noah's half-brother from before Scott met Bonnie."

Papa let out a wicked laugh. "Who knew Scott was such a player?"

Mama smiled, revealing a row of white false teeth. "What does Bonnie think about that?"

"She's fine with it."

Mama stood and pressed her stomach near the camera. "Is Bonnie still thinner than me?"

I replied, "Probably not after all the good food we've been eating at the castle."

Mama sat and waved her hands like a fan in a storm. "Only Italian people know how to cook."

"I think you'd like a lot of the food here," I said.

"What do they serve?" Mama asked.

"Fish, lamb, root vegetables, and haggis—their traditional food."

Papa rubbed his large stomach. "What's haggis?"

"Sheep organs, oatmeal, and spices cooked in a sheep's intestines."

Mama said, "I'd rather count sheep at night than eat them."

"I'll stick with manicotti," Papa said. "And pignolata, pizzella, and biscotti."

I smiled. "How's everything at the bakery?"

"Busy. We've been working into the night." Papa's thick gray eyebrows raised to his forehead. "Yesterday I was so tired I woke up and put toothpaste inside the cannoli."

"Now everyone in Kansas has clean teeth," Mama said with a chuckle.

I let out a half-hearted giggle.

"What's wrong, Nicky?" Mama asked.

"What's *wrong*, Mama?" Dad bit the side of his hand. "What do you think is wrong? Our son hasn't solved the murder mystery yet."

I did a doubletake to my screen. "How do you know there's been murders here in Scotland, Papa?"

"How do I *know*?" Papa laughed as if watching a standup comic. "Murder follows you everywhere."

"That's what Tony said."

"And he's right." Papa added, "Though he left us to become a Broadway choreographer, which incidentally is *your* fault."

"I know. Tony told me."

Papa grinned. "I also know about the murders, because our grandson mentioned them when he Skyped us."

Mama beamed like Rudolph the reindeer. "Our little Taavi was so happy to finally do a role-play for your investigation."

"He's some little actor, my grandson." Papa fastened the belt of his black robe. "You should have let him help you on a case sooner."

Taavi agrees with you.

"And I can't wait to see Taavi in the new movie. When is it coming out?" Mama asked.

"I'm not sure yet," I said with my mind wondering to the murders.

"Is Marcello Mastroianni in it?" Mama asked.

"Mama, he's been dead for centuries!" Papa rubbed his Roman nose. "Listen, Nicky, when your movie plays in our mall in Kansas, tell them to put it in the theatre with the stadium seating. The reclining chairs are so comfortable."

"Papa nods off at the opening credits," Mama said.

"While you play in the lobby arcade," Papa replied.

Ignoring him, Mama said, "Nicky, when you win an Academy Award and thank us, make sure you mention Abbondanza Bakery in Kansas." After a pause, she said, "Nicky? Are you still with us?"

"Sorry, Mama. I was thinking about my case."

Papa asked, "What has you stumped, son?"

Happy to get it off my chest, I said, "Somebody is murdering the members of the Conall family."

"What are the motives?" Papa asked like Sherlock Holmes's father.

I replied, "The usual: greed, revenge, jealousy, resentment."

"Who are the suspects?" Mama asked like an Italian Miss Marple.

"That's the point. I don't think any of the suspects did it."

"Then who did it?" Mama and Papa said in unison.

Maybe it's a family thing.

"That's what I can't figure out." I slid to the edge of my seat. "I know there is something I'm not seeing. And it's right under my nose."

"You questioned everyone and pretended to be other people to find out all the clues and suspects?" Mama asked.

"Yes."

"And you wrote down the suspects and motives?" Papa asked.

I nodded. "But I still came up empty."

"Then there's only one thing left to do." Papa said like Hercule Poirot, "Go over everything in your head that has happened to you this week. Hear every word everyone has said. And not said."

Of course! How could I have forgotten?

"And then nab the killer!" Mama added with gusto.

I kissed the screen. "I love you, Mama and Papa. You both helped me."

"Sure." Mama winked at me. "We're the parents of the great detective."

"Give everyone our love, son," Papa said.

"Except for the murderer. Love you!" Mama signed off.

So did I. A loud rumbling sound filled the room. *Do they have earthquakes in Scotland?* I realized it was my stomach. Salvation came with a knock on my door. After opening it, I found a lunch tray on the floor. *My husband is a saint! And room service is a miracle.* Scooping it up like a miner finding gold, I hurried back inside my room, placed the tray on my bed, and chowed down the stuffed mushrooms like a prisoner of war. The vegetables, herbs, pine nuts, and cheese melted in my mouth along with the savory mushroom caps. My vitamins and milk thistle capsules followed, chased down by an apple and yogurt smoothie.

Though my stomach was full, my mind was empty. I closed my laptop, put it away, and headed out the door. After making my way down the long staircase, I breezed through the hallway, and out the front door. I squinted in the warm sunlight as I crossed the stone bridge and walked on the cobblestone walkway. The gorgeous blue sky was dotted with puffs of white cotton as I continued my hike passing emerald-green meadows and hills in the distance. The fresh air cleared my mind. As Papa reminded me, I played back everything that had happened during our time in Scotland. Each person's voice reverberated in my head and their words permeated my consciousness. *That's it! How could I have not seen it? I know the identity of the murderer! Thank you, Papa!*

I ran as fast as I could along the road until the old abbey appeared in the distance. After arriving, I hurried up the stone steps, yanked open the door, and entered the hallway. It took a moment for my eyes to adjust to the lack of light. "Ewan!"

He appeared before me like an apparition. "What did you bring me, Nicky?" The ancient man smiled at me with devilish eyes.

"I think you know why I'm here."

"Aye." Approaching me, Ewan said, "Ye figured it out then, did ye?"

"I think so." *Stay calm. Keep breathing.* I took a step backward. "I had been focusing on your relationship with Emilia years ago."

"Aye."

"But what I should have been asking about was her husband, Kendric Conall."

"He were a workaholic. Always in his office, he were."

"So you said. And that's how I figured it all out."

"What do ye want with me?"

"I need you to answer something for me."

"Aye?"

I asked Ewan my question, and he confirmed what I had suspected.

"Thank you, Ewan."

The elderly man rested a wrinkled hand on his tiny hip. "Next time, bring me a gift, lad."

"I will."

The moment I got back outside, I began running toward to the castle. Suddenly, it felt as if my stomach dropped to my knees. I stopped and bent over to catch my breath. When I stood up, I felt like a passenger on a cruise whose eyeglasses had gone overboard. After a few deep breaths, I felt somewhat better. Picking up the pace, I continued along the cobblestone walkway.

I made my way across the stone bridge and over the moat, unable to shake my feeling of nausea. *Lairie. I have to find Lairie!* After yanking open the heavy castle door, I walked through the entryway. Though out of breath, I pushed myself to hurry up the stairs.

Arriving at Brody and Lairie's room, I knocked on the door. Receiving no answer, I tried the brass knob and found the door open. Feeling queasy, I ran in and collapsed onto the sofa. *Where is Lairie?*

The door opened, and Chief Inspector Lennox Frazier entered the room.

"Where's Lairie?"

His chubby face began circling around the room. "I've taken care of everything."

"Lairie—"

Darkness.

I woke belly flat on a cold, stone floor. Peering upward, I noticed the black room was empty except for small barred windows (from the outside). The only furniture in the room—a wide bench—seemed to be floating in midair. "Where am I?"

"The dungeon room of course." Frazier sat on the bench.

I staggered to sit upright. The nausea was fierce, and my stomach was on fire. "What did you put in my lunch?"

"Poisonous mushrooms. All mushrooms in Scotland are edible, but some only once!" He giggled like spoiled child.

"Where is Lairie?"

"I found her with your family, eating lunch in the Great Hall. In my role as chief inspector, I called her away for an interview in the library. Then I pushed the little lassie into the hidden room you used in your movie, tied her up, taped her mouth shut, and sealed the door. She'll eventually die from suffocation or starvation." He guffawed.

"Then you'll make your case for ownership of Conall

Castle."

"Good work, amateur detective. I knew I could count on you."

I rested my elbows on my knees and supported my aching head with my shaking hands. "How much time do I have?"

"I wouldn't tell a long story." He chuckled.

I need to keep him talking while Noah tries to find me. "How did you know that I figured it out?"

"During your first two visits with Ewan Baird, I hid outside under an abbey window. I realized it was only a matter of time."

"Don't you want to know how I put the pieces of the puzzle together?"

"We're playing a puzzle game, are we?" The husky man stared down at me. "All right. We have nothing else to do while we wait for you to leave the living. Let's hear it, Nicky."

I looked up at Frazier's floating face. "A few people mentioned that when Kendric Conall was alive he spent all his time working in the office at the castle. Seems that Ewan and Emilia took advantage of that in the abbey, and Fergus was the result." I rubbed my forehead in an unsuccessful attempt to ease my headache. "You mentioned to me that your mother was Kendric's bookkeeper, and he kept her long hours. Just this morning, Ewan confirmed for me that Kendric and Elsbeth weren't always working during that time. Ewan had spied on them and found out they had had an affair. I took the leap that Kendric was your real father."

"Correct, Professor. I am impressed. Go on."

"Since Kendric wanted to raise Fergus as his own son to avoid a scandal three years earlier, I'm guessing he paid off your mother and father to keep quiet about his paternity of *you*."

"Good guess!"

"And I'm also guessing you found out about it

somehow."

He moved the mop of brown hair off his forehead. "On my mother's death bed, a year ago. She finally spilled the beans. Like Kendric had spilled the seed thirty years before." Frazier cackled wildly.

He's clearly insane. "And that started your plan into action." I took in a few deep breaths, so I wouldn't vomit from the nausea. "Like Brody and Lairie Naughton, you considered the Conalls to be bullies and tyrants. Kendric worked your mother to an early death and kept you a secret bastard (*pun intended*). You wanted to rip the silver spoons out of their mouths and take your true place as laird of Conall Castle. So, you killed Kendric and Emilia, placed them in their car, and drove it off the cliff's edge into the sea." *Where is Noah?*

"I'm impressed, Nicky! You really are good at this."

"Hearing about my movie, I believe you came up with the idea to mimic the murders in the film and then pin them on me—as a deranged movie director unable to tell reality from reel." *Is his face moving from corner to corner in the room?* "So, you adapted your bumbling chief inspector act, citing nepotism as how you got your position— thanks to your presumed father, the deceased Chief Superintendent."

He smirked. "I am a bit on the clumsy side actually, but not quite the galoot you witnessed. But it was so much fun to play!" He chortled hysterically.

"You pushed Barclay off that cliff into the sea, stabbed Magnus with the knight's sword, pushed Fergus and Moira off the bridge into the alligator moat, and poisoned Fergus with sweet-smelling antifreeze and then placed his body inside the armor. Before I had figured it all out, I phoned you about Lairie. Instead of sending over an officer as you had promised, you took your cue and sealed her away in the hidden room." *I have more tremors than an active volcano during an earthquake.* "You probably wore gloves or tampered with the DNA testing results so none of your DNA would be found on any of the victims. Even if it were, as chief inspector, you could have claimed you were simply examining the bodies."

"Aren't I a clever lad?" Frazier giggled like a child poisoning a pet frog.

"Clever? You killed seven people and locked up two more—all out of greed and vengeance."

As if transforming into the theatre masks, his jovial face instantly switched to one of rage, disgust, and homicidal mania. "Kendric stole my mother away from my father. He kept her locked up in that office until all hours." He groaned. "Until she let down her guard. Then when she had his child, he disowned me. And he forced her to keep the secret that I was a Conall with the same birthright as his spoiled, selfish, arrogant, good-for-nothing sons." He darted around the room like a grasshopper. *Or am I hallucinating?* "Barclay couldn't keep it in his pants. Magnus was a thief. Fergus was a drunk, a gambler, and a rapist." He pounded his hand against his chest. "All of them put together weren't half the man I am." Tears filled his wild eyes. "Why didn't Kendric see that? He was my father. Why didn't he realize that *I* should be his heir?" He wept bitterly.

The room spun around me like a top on a Ferris wheel. "Did the Chief Superintendent love you?"

Frazier roared with laughter that turned into tears of sadness running down his cheeks. "Balloch knew I wasn't his son. So he treated me like a visiting distant relative. Even when I followed in his footsteps and became an inspector, I was never good enough for him."

Feeling weaker, I lay on my side in the fetal position. *Come fast, Noah. I can't hold on much longer.* "He didn't die of a heart attack a few years ago, did he?"

"Balloch had a heart condition all right. But *I* had his medicines. And one night, *he* didn't!" He jumped up and down in erratic laughter. "Like a flower in a dark, dry room seeking water or sunlight, I watched Balloch die calling for his medicine. Just like I'm watching you die now, Nicky. In my investigation notes, I had planned to write, 'How could an American be expected to know a safe mushroom from a poisonous one?' But it's taking too long, and I'm tired of waiting." Frazier raised the sole of his foot over my face. "It's time for your final exit, Nicky. As I enter as laird of Conall Castle."

"Get your sole off my husband. The only thing you'll be entering is a prison cell." Noah burst in and pointed to Frazier. "Deflower him, Owen!"

Inspector Owen Steward yanked Frazier to his feet and applied the handcuffs. "I suspected Lennox, I mean the Chief Inspector for quite some time. My lovestruck act, for the most part, was a way to stay on top of him." He winked. "If you know what I mean, Professor."

Noah used his cell phone to call for an ambulance.

Taavi hurried to my side, knelt down, and placed his small hand on my shoulder. "When you weren't at lunch, Dad started to worry. We searched all over the castle. Then I remembered playing in the dungeon with Lairie. Nobody else ever comes down here. So I thought the murderer might have thrown you down here to trap you."

I somehow managed to get out, "Lairie's in the hidden room."

"I know. When we were searching for you, I went to the hallway of the hidden room and heard Lairie's moans for help. Dad used a sword to unseal the room and get her out." Taavi grinned proudly. "She's making me first knight of the castle."

Noah kneeled at my other side and supported my head on his chest. "Stay with me, honey."

"Always. You're my savior, Noah."

"And you're mine."

I heard the ambulance as I kissed Noah's neck and the

room went dark.

EPILOGUE

A week later, I stood at the entrance to the shining clean castle ballroom. The crystal chandeliers lined the tall ceiling, and the flowing burgundy velvet curtains flanked the colossal windows towering over window seats positioned all over the enormous room. I admired the white stone fireplaces standing majestically at the center of each of the four walls, and the burgundy velvet sofas, chaises, and easy chairs throughout the space. Finally, I smiled at the pink and white Scottish roses filling the chamber, along with various guests dressed in suits and gowns.

Four men in traditional Scottish attire entered through the massive oak doors with bagpipes in hand. The glorious sound filled my ears as the men made their way to an elevated corner of the ballroom.

Next, Lairie Naughton, the owner of Conall Castle, made her way to the stage area with her white gown flowing behind her as she dropped sweet-smelling flower petals along the way.

My son, Taavi Kapuli Oliver Abbondanza was next, wearing a black tuxedo with a burgundy ruffled shirt that matched the large pillow he carried to transport two golden wedding bands.

After Taavi walked up the steps to the raised area, Best Men Noah and yours truly entered arm in arm and took our places on each side of the dais.

The bagpipe music heightened, and the crowd cheered

as Mom, wearing a gorgeous peach gown, ushered Donal Blair into the room and up the stairs.

The applause continued as Dad (actually wearing a tuxedo!) led Brody Naughton through the room and to Brody's place on the stage next to Donal. Then Dad joined Mom on one side of the platform.

In their blue-and-white plaid tunics, kilts, sporran, long hose, brogues, and cloaks, the grooms gazed at each other lovingly.

The officiate, Chief Inspector Owen Stewart, took his place between them. "We are gathered here together to celebrate the marriage of Brody Naughton and Donal Blair. Who gives away Brody?"

Dad blinked back tears. "I do. His father."

Owen nodded. "And who gives away Donal?"

"I do. His soon-to-be mother-in-law." Mom kissed Donal's cheek. "And I'm a good mother-in-law. Aren't I Nicky?"

I winked at her.

"And who stands up for these two lads?" Owen asked.

Noah moved next to Brody. "I am Brody's brother."

"And I'm Donal's soon-to-be brother-in-law." I proudly took my place next to Donal.

Owen gazed out at the crowd. "Does anyone here have any cause to object to these two lads getting married. And you better not, since I'm the law in this county and I won't have any of it."

The crowd roared with laughter.

"Will the grooms say their piece." Owen nodded to Brody and Donal.

Brody took Donal's hand. "Donal, you turned a brute into a man, a cold hearth into a fiery furnace, and a child into an adult. You are my friend, my love, and my partner forever."

Donal wiped the tears from his cheeks. "I loved you from the first moment I met you. And I never stopped. And it wasn't always easy."

The audience chuckled.

"But it *is* incredibly easy and right forming a family with you and Lairie," Donal said.

Lairie blew them a kiss.

Donal added, "I couldn't ask for a better husband, daughter, and in-laws."

Mom took a picture of Brody and Lairie, texted, and whispered to me, "Judy wishes Tommy and Timmy's wedding had been in a Scottish castle with Dung on the flowers."

"Now for the ancient Celtic blessing." Owen placed a hand on the grooms' shoulders. "May you both be blessed with the strength of heaven, the light of the sun, the radiance of the moon, the splendor of fire, the speed of lightning, the depth of the sea, the swiftness of wind, the stability of earth, and the firmness of rock." He handed each of them a Celtic medal. "Lads, take strength from the sea, majesty from the mountains, souring from the cliffs, and tranquility from the moors. You are no longer one but two. Joined in love and life until death do you part, and after with your ancestors in the heavens."

Owen nodded to Taavi, and our son handed the rings to the grooms. Brody and Donal placed the bands on each other's fingers. Owen said, "You may now kiss."

Brody and Donal threw their arms around each other and shared a long kiss to the guests' delight.

"You are now husbands for life."

The audience erupted in deafening applause.

I patted his small back. "Congratulations, Donal!"

"Lucky me," Donal said. "I not only get a terrific husband, amazing daughter, and stunning castle; I married into the most wonderful family."

I couldn't disagree.

Noah bear-hugged Brody. "Congratulations, brother."

"I really meant that about staying in touch," Brody

said.

"So did I," Noah replied.

Mom and Dad chimed in with, "And we'll keep you to it!"

Lairie made her way to the center of the platform and addressed the crowd. "As the new mistress of Conall Castle, I promise every one of you that my wonderful dads and I will treat every employee, guest, and neighbor with compassion, honor, and welcome. Conall Castle is no longer a place of dark clouds, anger, and resentment. This castle, and all the property around it, is now a place of joy, celebration, and love!"

The giant room filled with rapturous applause. Ewan Baird, in his usual work clothes, stood in a corner of the room. He raised a bottle of whiskey to me and smiled. I nodded back.

Lairie walked over to Taavi. "I'm really glad we're cousins, Taavi."

"Me too," Taavi replied. "But I'm not only your cousin. I'm also the first knight to the mistress of the castle."

They shared a conspiratorial giggle.

Noah pulled me over to a corner of the room. "The newlyweds make me remember *our* wedding, Nicky."

"I'll never forget it." I kissed the soft lips of the man of my dreams. "And thank you for saving me again, Noah."

"I'll always have your back."

"And I'll always have yours."

We shared a devilish smile.

Taavi joined us. "I saved you too, Pop."

"You sure did. You're becoming a regular detective, son," I said.

Noah nodded. "Looks like we have some competition, Nicky."

"And some help." Taavi offered us the hang loose sign. "This was a good Nicky and Noah *and Taavi* mystery."

Martin and Ruben, in matching chartreuse tuxedos,

made their way over to us.

"Wasn't that a beautiful wedding?" Noah asked them.

"Yes, but not as touching and beautiful as my screenplay." Martin nudged my side. "Nicky, we need to get back to Vermont tomorrow to start editing our film!"

Ruben grinned like a fox in a locked henhouse. "Public television is interested in airing it."

Taavi lit up like a neon sign surrounded by sparklers. "This might lead to my own public television show!"

That's our boy.

While the orchestra set up for the dancing to come, we all followed the crowd out of the ballroom toward the Great Hall for a sumptuous buffet.

"Come on, Martin." Ruben grabbed his arm. "I want to be first on line at the buffet, so I can eat and go to bed at a decent hour."

Martin followed his husband. "I miss the old days when I danced until dawn and then wrote of my suitors in my diary."

"Nostalgic for the hieroglyphics, Martin?" said Ruben.

As we walked, Noah said, "Nicky, be sure to have your milk thistle capsules after dinner."

"Why?" I asked.

Noah replied, "The doctor said it helped counteract the effects of the poisonous mushrooms. That and the stomach pump."

"The pump I remember."

"You think you'd be accustomed to that by now, Pop." Taavi came between us, took our hands, and led us to our usual table at the Great Hall. We were truly three lairds of the castle.

About the Author

Bestselling author **Joe Cosentino** was voted Favorite LGBT Mystery, Humorous, and Contemporary Author of the Year by the readers of Divine Magazine for *Drama Queen*. He also wrote the other novels in the Nicky and Noah mystery series: *Drama Muscle, Drama Cruise, Drama Luau, Drama Detective, Drama Fraternity, Drama Castle, Drama Dance*; the Dreamspinner Press novellas: *In My Heart/An Infatuation & A Shooting Star*, the Bobby and Paolo Holiday Stories: *A Home for the Holidays/The Perfect Gift/The First Noel, The Naked Prince and Other Tales from Fairyland* with *Holiday Tales from Fairyland*; the Cozzi Cove series: *Cozzi Cove: Bouncing Back, Cozzi Cove: Moving Forward, Cozzi Cove: Stepping Out, Cozzi Cove: New Beginnings, Cozzi Cove: Happy Endings* (NineStar Press); and the Jana Lane mysteries: *Paper Doll, Porcelain Doll, Satin Doll, China Doll, Rag Doll* (The Wild Rose Press). He has appeared in principal acting roles in film, television, and theatre, opposite stars such as Bruce Willis, Rosie O'Donnell, Nathan Lane, Holland Taylor, and Jason Robards. Joe is currently Chair of the Department/Professor at a college in upstate New York and is happily married. Joe was voted 2nd Place Favorite LGBT Author of the Year in Divine Magazine's Readers' Choice Awards, and his books have received numerous Favorite Book of the Month Awards and Rainbow Award Honorable Mentions.

Connect with this author on social media

Web site: http://www.JoeCosentino.weebly.com
Facebook: http://www.facebook.com/JoeCosentinoauthor
Twitter: https://twitter.com/JoeCosen
Amazon: http://Author.to/JoeCosentino
Goodreads: https://www.goodreads.com/author/show/4071647.Joe_Cosentino

And don't miss any of the Nicky and Noah mysteries by Joe Cosentino

DRAMA QUEEN

It could be curtains for college theatre professor Nicky Abbondanza. With dead bodies popping up all over campus, Nicky must use his drama skills to figure out who is playing the role of murderer before it is lights out for Nicky and his colleagues. Complicating matters is Nicky's huge crush on Noah Oliver, a gorgeous assistant professor in his department, who may or may not be involved with Nicky's cocky graduate assistant and is also the top suspect for the murders! You will be applauding and shouting Bravo for Joe Cosentino's fast-paced, side-splittingly funny, edge-of-your-seat, delightfully entertaining novel. Curtain up!

Winner of *Divine Magazine*'s Readers' Poll Awards as Favorite LGBT Mystery, Crime, Humorous, and Contemporary novel of 2015!

DRAMA MUSCLE

It could be lights out for college theatre professor Nicky Abbondanza. With dead bodybuilders popping up on campus, Nicky, and his favorite colleague/life partner Noah Oliver, must use their drama skills to figure out who is taking down pumped up musclemen in the Physical Education building before it is curtain down for Nicky and Noah. Complicating matters is a visit from Noah's parents from Wisconsin, and Nicky's suspicion that Noah may be hiding more than a cut, smooth body. You will be applauding and shouting Bravo for Joe Cosentino's fast-paced, side-splittingly funny, edge-of-your-seat entertaining second novel in this delightful series. Curtain up and weights up!

2015-2016 Rainbow Award Honorable Mention

DRAMA CRUISE

Theatre professors and couple, Nicky Abbondanza and Noah Oliver, are going overboard as usual, but this time on an Alaskan cruise, where dead college theatre professors are popping up everywhere from the swimming pool to the captain's table. Further complicating matters are Nicky's and Noah's parents as surprise cruise passengers, and Nicky's assignment to direct a murder mystery dinner theatre show onboard ship. Nicky and Noah will need to use their drama skills to figure out who is bringing the curtain down on vacationing theatre professors before it is lights out for the handsome couple. You will be applauding and shouting Bravo for Joe Cosentino's fast-paced, side-splittingly funny, edge-of-your-seat entertaining third novel in this delightful series. Curtain up and ship ahoy!

DRAMA DETECTIVE

Theatre professor Nicky Abbondanza is directing *Sherlock Holmes, the Musical* in a professional summer stock production at Treemeadow College, co-starring his husband and theatre professor colleague, Noah Oliver, as Dr. John Watson. When cast members begin toppling over like hammy actors at a curtain call, Nicky dons Holmes' persona onstage and off. Once again Nicky and Noah will need to use their drama skills to figure out who is lowering the street lamps on the actors before the handsome couple get half-baked on Baker Street. You will be applauding and shouting Bravo for Joe Cosentino's fast-paced, side-splittingly funny, edge-of-your-seat entertaining fifth novel in this delightful series. Curtain up, the game is afoot!

Drama Fraternity

Theatre professor Nicky Abbondanza is directing *Tight End Scream Queen*, a slasher movie filmed at Treemeadow College's football fraternity house, co-starring his husband and theatre professor colleague, Noah Oliver. When young hunky cast members begin fading out with their scenes, Nicky and Noah will once again need to use their drama skills to figure out who is sending the quarterback, jammer, wide receiver, and more to the cutting room floor before Nicky and Noah hit the final reel. You will be applauding and shouting Bravo for Joe Cosentino's fast-paced, side-splittingly funny, edge-of-your-seat entertaining sixth novel in this delightful series. Lights, camera, action, frat house murders!

Drama Castle

Theatre professor Nicky Abbondanza is directing a historical film at a castle in Scotland, co-starring his spouse, theatre professor Noah Oliver, and their son Taavi. When historical accuracy disappears along with hunky men in kilts, Nicky and Noah will once again need to use their drama skills to figure out who is pitching residents of Conall Castle off the drawbridge and into the moat, before Nicky and Noah land in the dungeon. You will be applauding and shouting Bravo for Joe Cosentino's fast-paced, side-splittingly funny, edge-of-your-seat entertaining seventh novel in this delightful series. Take your seats. The curtain is going up on steep cliffs, ancient turrets, stormy seas, misty moors, malfunctioning kilts, and murder!

Coming soon:

DRAMA DANCE

Theatre professor Nicky Abbondanza is back at Treemeadow College directing their Nutcracker Ballet co-starring his spouse, theatre professor Noah Oliver, their son Taavi, and their best friend and department head, Martin Anderson. With muscular dance students and faculty in the cast, the Christmas tree on stage isn't the only thing rising. When cast members drop faster than their loaded dance belts, Nicky and Noah will once again need to use their drama skills to figure out who is cracking the Nutcracker's nuts, trapping the Mouse King, and being cavalier with the Cavalier, before Nicky and Noah end up stuck in the Land of the Sweets. You will be applauding and shouting Bravo for Joe Cosentino's fast-paced, side-splittingly funny, edge-of-your-seat entertaining eighth novel in this delightful series. Take your seats. The curtain is going up on the Fairy—Sugar Plum that is, clumsy mice, malfunctioning toys, and murder!

Drama Faerie

It's summer at Treemeadow College's new Globe Theatre, where theatre professor Nicky Abbondanza is directing a musical production of *A Midsummer Night's Dream* co-starring his spouse, theatre professor Noah Oliver, their son Taavi, and their best friend and department head, Martin Anderson. With an all-male, skimpily dressed cast and a love potion gone wild, romance is in the starry night air. When hunky students and faculty in the production drop faster than their tunics and tights, Nicky and Noah will need to use their drama skills to figure out who is taking swordplay to the extreme before Nicky and Noah end up foiled in the forest. You will be applauding and shouting Bravo for Joe Cosentino's fast-paced, side-splittingly funny, edge-of-your-seat entertaining ninth novel in this delightful series. Take your seats. The curtain is going up on star-crossed young lovers, a faerie queen, an ass who is a great Bottom, and murder!

Drama Runway

It's spring break at Treemeadow College, and theatre professor Nicky Abbondanza is directing a runway show for the Fashion Department. Joining him are his spouse, theatre professor Noah Oliver, their son Taavi, and their best friend and department head, Martin Anderson. Designed by visiting professor Ulla Ultimate, the show is bound to be the ultimate event of the season. And bound it is with designs featuring black leather and chains. When sexy male models drop faster than their leather chaps, Nicky and Noah will need to use their drama skills to figure out who is taking the term "a cut male model" literally before Nicky and Noah end up steamed in the wardrobe steamer. You will be applauding and shouting Bravo for Joe Cosentino's fast-paced, side-splittingly funny, edge-of-your-seat entertaining tenth novel in this delightful series. Take your seats. The runway is lighting up with hunky models, volatile designers, bitter exes, newfound lovers, and murder!

Drama Christmas

It's winter holiday time at Treemeadow College, and Theatre Professor Nicky Abbondanza, his husband Theatre Associate Professor Noah Oliver, their son Taavi, and best friends Martin and Ruben are donning their gay apparel in a musical version of Scrooge's *A Christmas Carol*, entitled *Call Me Carol!* More than stockings are hung when hunky chorus members drop like snowflakes. Once again, our favorite thespians will need to use their drama skills to catch the killer and make the yuletide gay before their Christmas balls get cracked. You will be applauding and shouting Bravo for Joe Cosentino's fast-paced, side-splittingly funny, edge-of-your-seat entertaining eleventh novel in this delightful series. Take your seats. The stage lights are coming up on an infamous miser, S&M savvy ghost, Victorian lovers of the past, present, and future, a not so Tiny Tim, and murder!

Books by Joe Cosentino

The Nicky and Noah Comedy Mystery Series:
Drama Queen
Drama Muscle
Drama Cruise
Drama Luau
Drama Detective
Drama Fraternity
Drama Castle
Drama Dance (coming soon)
Drama Faerie (coming soon)
Drama Runway (coming soon)
Drama Christmas (coming soon)

The Cozzi Cove series (NineStar Press):
Cozzi Cove: Bouncing Back
Cozzi Cove: Moving Forward
Cozzi Cove: Stepping Out
Cozzi Cove: New Beginnings
Cozzi Cove: Happy Endings

The Dreamspinner Press novellas:
IN MY HEART: An Infatuation & A Shooting Star
TALES FROM FAIRYLAND: The Naked Prince and Other Tales from Fairyland and *Holiday Tales from Fairyland*
BOBBY AND PAOLO HOLIDAY STORIES: A Home for the Holidays; The Perfect Gift; and *The First Noel*

The Jana Lane Mysteries:
Paper Doll
Porcelain Doll (The Wild Rose Press)
Satin Doll (The Wild Rose Press)
China Doll (The Wild Rose Press)
Rag Doll (The Wild Rose Press)

37301945R00116

Made in the USA
Middletown, DE
24 February 2019